Mental House

Mental House

The Roman Opening

MENT

iUniverse, Inc.
New York Lincoln Shanghai

Mental House
The Roman Opening

Copyright © 2006 by Charles Anthony Ancium

iUniverse books may be ordered through booksellers or by contacting:

iUniverse
2021 Pine Lake Road, Suite 100
Lincoln, NE 68512
www.iuniverse.com
1-800-Authors (1-800-288-4677)

ISBN-13: 978-0-595-38579-9 (pbk)
ISBN-13: 978-0-595-82960-6 (cloth)
ISBN-13: 978-0-595-82958-3 (ebk)
ISBN-10: 0-595-38579-6 (pbk)
ISBN-10: 0-595-82960-0 (cloth)
ISBN-10: 0-595-82958-9 (ebk)

Printed in the United States of America

ACKNOWLEDGEMENTS

Peace and Wisdom. I would like to thank God, *my belated mother,* Ernestine Ancrum. May God keep her protected in the after life. My mother will always be the strongest woman I had the pleasure of knowing. Love and happiness to Ezekiel and Ruby Ancrum. God's grace to Corey K. Ancrum. My belated grandmother Dorothy Ancrum, and my Grandfather Ezekiel Ancrum, I love you. I'll never be too old to tell you that. Also, love to my new cousin Bryanna Amyra Grice. I thank my brother Roman Felix, for coming out to NYC and giving the creative material with your spirited antics. God bless you and the fams. Very special thanks to Vanessa Griffith, who has always been my best friend. Don't change.

I would like to thank my Commander Col. Carskadon, for enhancing my qualities as a leader. I would also like to thank Jody-Lynn Davis, the chess playing RN, for mentoring me in my mission to be a higher-level nurse. Erika Keaton, thanks for being the truth! I am blessed to know phenomenal women.

I want to thank Tyrone Smith for being my chess mentor. Thank you Noel Williams, for all of your wisdom and support that keeps me focused. Let's market our diets! Dorian Jean and Family, congratulations on the new addition to the family.

A special thank you to Mrs. Mercedes and her staff for their unconditional love and support. Book signing at Mercedes Lounge!

I would like to thank Fritz, the underground artist for the lessons that made me a better writer. I want to thank the brothers and sisters of Woodhull hospital. A special thanks to psych unit 3. We put the hood in Wood hull (just joking).

If you liked the book, please let me know by addressing the mail to Pieceslayers address. If you did not like it…please address your comments to Subvidious's address. (Again, just kidding!)

All of you that were not addressed personally, I would still like to express my sincere thank you for being a part of my life. Also, thank you for your support.

I am offering my readers a little poetry to end the book on a gentle note. I hope you *feel me.*

Chapter I

Fluorescent lighting flickered uncontrollably on the ninth floor, adjacent to staircase "A" in the Panama building, Lefrak City. Jessie, the chief electrical custodian, troubleshot the circuitry. She even replaced the entire unit, but could not seem to repair the fixture. Neighbors believe that a spirit of protection remains restless on this floor. The wisdom also spoke of a young child that walks with an old soul.

"That eh, eh, nino walkin' this place before, comprende. You leesten to him," Mrs. Mayra spanglished her way into conversation, as she continued to knit from the balls of yarn embedded in her purse disguised as a colorful department store shopping bag.

"I wonder how *you* listen to him Mrs. Mayra, the boy speaks English...heh, heh," Joe chuckled matter-of-factly in his normal antisocial manner, his eyes rolled, head turned away and legs crossed as he sat alone on the adjacent bench.

"Shut up ya old goat! She speaks well enough to sit here and entertain your broke ass. Always askin' for a quarter...And what are you gonna do with a quarter? Nothing but ask for another one," Mable retorts rolling her eyes right back at him, defending her friend of five years.

"That boy is the devil," Joe ignores Mable and responds to Mrs. Mayra.

"What chu talkin' about Joe?" Mrs. Mayra says.

"I heard him speaking to you the other day about some dream. When he finished telling you the dream, I'll be damned if you didn't go straight to the number man and hit the number straight for seven hundred dollars! Now, *that's* the devil!"

"That ain't no devil to me. That's an angel!" Mable says as she slaps Mrs. Mayra five.

There is something special about this young man. He has walked this earth before; he has traveled through his dreams. His dreams cause concern...but strangely, they speak the truth. The young man they speak of is Roman Phoenix; and the spirit that disturbs the lights in the buildings...it is his guardian Angel, Sirius. Sirius is a soul without rest. He must bring restitution to those spirits haunting Roman's dreams. Roman's dreams reveal the truth. Although the essence of truth is pure, oftentimes the content of the truth is wicked. This curse of receiving the revelations has him in impending danger. Sirius, his Angel ascertains that the supernatural does not ingest him as he travels.

I am about to tell a story…a story of my dreams…

I am Roman Phoenix, a ten year old kid. But I have been told that I have an old soul. I guess they mean I am intelligent for my age. I'm cool with that.

I'm going to read to you the last entry in my journal. These entries are written for my psychiatrist, he thinks it will help my disorder. Please accept my mistakes for love and my eloquence as the spirit that moves within me. (I don't know, but it sounds good in church)…ehmm ehmm…As I awake from the haunted dreams that hold me captive, it is like the abrupt end to the refueling of my mind, body, and spirit. I cue my mental microphone in preparation for the day ahead, making sure that the report of my saga is received without confusion.

I wrote that. Cool, huh? Anyways…I'm in the fifth grade, and I'm in the e-track. The e-track is short for the excel track. It is for the kids that have performed outstandingly in their previous grade.

My mom says that there's something special about me. My teacher, Mrs. Adaire says that too. Although Mrs. Adaire sometimes calls me a nudnik when I do something silly, I get the feeling she likes me. Maybe she just thinks that I am short bus special. It's hard to tell.

Mrs. Adaire was the type of teacher that even when she was not in school you could guess she was a teacher. You knew the type…hair always up, glasses, had the aura of being all-knowing, nurturing when she needed to be and strict when she had to be…which was almost all of the time. Oh, did I mention she was ugly? She gave my brother an unsatisfactory on his report card a few years back because he said she looked like flava flav in a wig. Her face was like whoa! I would go on, but I think you get the point.

Ms. Adaire became the school chess coach by default. She introduced the idea to the faculty, and after a brief discussion, they asked her to organize the team. She knew nothing about chess, but quickly learned after spending much of her free time going to competitions and getting lessons from the masters of the game.

My brother thinks that I was adopted, because I do things that no one else in the family does. Like when I *know* that I touch something, I have to touch it with the other hand. If by some chance I can't make it happen, I become very nervous and I can't concentrate. I know…it *is* crazy, I just can't help it!

I was lucky, my bad…I mean blessed. My mom always said there is no such thing as luck, only blessings. I was blessed to have a brother who played chess well. He taught me how to play. I was the second best on my team, thanks to my big brother. Being very competitive, he would challenge me anytime he saw me in my chess shirt or uniform. He never allowed me to win a game. But as he continued to beat me, I learned.

My classmates call me weird Roman, or Roman the weirdo. In the beginning, I hid my disorder well. I could not keep it hidden for long though, it would eventually get the best of me and rear its ugly head upon me. There were times I would be taking a test in class and Mrs. Adaire would hand me a pencil; it would be placed in my right hand. I would ask for another pencil in case one broke. It had nothing to do with the pencil breaking. It was so she could place a pencil in my other hand. If she would not oblige my subtle request, I was sure to fail. No matter how hard I studied or how well I prepared for the examination, this strange feeling would overcome me. For some strange reason I think Mrs. Adaire actually knew what I was going through. She knew everything. She punished me when I misbehaved, just as she punished the other classmates that misbehaved. She was a fair dean. She overlooked the things related to my strange behavior, even when it was brought to her attention by other teachers. Once my friends found out that I was bothered by this aberrancy, they would do all kinds of things to torture me. My best friend would wait until I slapped him five and then he would ask me did I want him to slap my other hand…*of course I did*, and he knew it. Smiling like a Cheshire cat, he would walk away and tell me to catch him. After two or three times of getting into trouble for running in the hallway, I just pretended that it no longer bothered me. However, on the inside, it drove me mad.

My mom took me to a team of professionals because it began to affect my grades. A psychiatrist, a psychologist, a behavioral therapist, and a mental health nurse. The psychiatrist diagnosed my disease as obsessive-compulsive personality disorder (OCD). He gave me some pills flux…fluox…hydro…well the short name is prozac. They made me feel like a zombie, and I had to go to counseling twice a week. One session was individual therapy and the other was family counseling, which helped a lot. Eventually, I no longer had to take the pills regularly. Although the disease did not go away, it did become manageable.

Thank God for the end of the week. I would not have to deal with my sadistic friends. Later in the evening, I would come home, eat, shower, and go to my room. My brother did not bother me as long as I did not bother him. He knew I was doing a cleansing ritual. In the family therapy group, he signed a contract promising that he would not interrupt my cleansing process. I began performing this ritual every night. It would "fix" all of the unevenness that I was subjected to during the day. With therapy, the rituals had been decreased to once a week. They would have something to do with a number that was on my mind during the episodes. I would have to touch both edges of my pillow with both hands, the number of times just before I went to bed. After the cleansing ritual was accomplished, I, although rather unsoundly, was able to sleep most of the night.

My mother drove me crazy as she tried to help me, as she did for every member of the household. I guess it had to do with her co-dependency. She had to help us with our problems, or else she would have a problem. It bothered her almost as it bothered me when I had an episode.

On the shelves in the living room, on the floor in neat piles, and even in the bathroom, there were a slew of books and journals on each person's sickness in the family. Alcoholism for my dad, co-dependency for my mom, and my OCD books. They were arranged in alphabetical order, thanks to yours truly. They were also arranged by genre, and furthermore, by disease. I would do strange things like this at home all the time. It balanced me. As I did these things to bring balance to my life, I would catch my mom staring at me as if I was a zoo animal. She would quickly look away after she took mental notes. She would then try her best to maintain the new habitat that I had arranged.

The first time that my brother was suspended, it was for fighting in school. He took it to this guy's body. Dad said that he would have went to juvie, if they could have proved that he started it. Everyone knew that my brother started it, but no one in my brother's class would go against him or his crew.

I was secretly elated. Not because he beat the guy up, but because he got caught. *Now he* had a problem, it was called conduct disorder, by the doctor. *Now he* would be enveloped with mom's secret recipes of how to be normal. *Now he* would have to spend extra time with mom and dad. *Now he* had to suffer talking to the psych and I could now call him the freakin' psycho he always called me. Although I said it to him many times in my head, I never got up enough courage to say it aloud. It still did not negate the fact that every time he said it to me, I thought to him…*you're, you're, you're the freakin psycho!* It made me smile…I would smile like I had teeth on my forehead. He never did get it…the reason that I would smile when he called me a psycho. He just thought I was weird. Personally, I didn't care. Mom brought some new books for him to read, some on conduct disorder, and others on anti-social behavior. She found a home for them in the living room, I was loving it.

Five o'clock arrived on a brisk Saturday September morning. My clock radio was blaring gospel music. I was relieved, because the alarm going off was the only way to escape the havoc causing nightmares. I cut it off as soon as it rang, careful not to disturb my brother in his sleep. I learned all too early never to wake a sleeping bear.

Looking out of the window, I caught a glimpse of the brightest star. Although the clouds attempt to hide it as it is buoyed by the sky, teetering on the edge of the horizon. Its brilliance was causing me to squint. The sun had been overzealous this particular morning.

In my neighborhood, the horns of the big delivery trucks sound off in their own harmony as they attempt to make their routes. The pizza guy argues with the person delivering the pizza products. Concurrently, Mrs. Garcia (Mrs. Mayra) on the third floor is yelling out the window for her husband to return to the apartment. He tries to ignore her, but she says something in Spanish, I did not understand it, but he surely did. He was afire with anger. As the neighbor's argument increased in intensity, so did the argument between the pizza guys. Although the pizza guy's argument had been vociferous, compared to the neighbors, their argument was barely audible.

Teenagers were assembled early in the morning waiting for the Waldbaum's across the street to open. They would pack the customers bags at the supermarket for spare change. Packing bags quickly became a street lesson for the delinquent youth. It was extortion 101. If the manager did not permit the rude boys to bag the groceries, the young punks would harass the employees. Even worse, they would harass the patrons.

Meanwhile, from the windowsill, I observe the ghetto fowl thug a woman out of her stale bread in the park. Joggers pick up their step in the park, with fictitious hopes of giving the muggers a disadvantage. Dog walkers and their pets rustle the leaves in the recreation area.

My eyes continue piercing out of the window, consuming life through sight, it was exhilarating. I took a deep breath. Now, I am wide-awake.

As I look around for the remote, I see that my brother has once again, ransacked the room that I clean up religiously every night before I go to bed. If the remote had been on the floor, I would never know it by just looking from the top of the bed. He placed his football jersey on my bed. I wondered why the smell of armpits conquered the smell of funky socks that usually filled the room when he went to bed. The rest of his gear is sprawled across the floor. Even if I find the remote, I still have to get up and remove his jacket from the screen to be able to watch anything. It didn't matter, because I never wanted to watch television. It was just a pawn in the game. I wanted to speak to my brother badly, but just as the alarm clock would cause my untimely death, so would the subtle, inconspicuous, turning on the television to awaken my brother. For now, I lie awake, looking out the window.

I am too displaced mentally to think about anything except what my mind has just dreamt. I must risk it. I have to share this series of dreams with him, or someone, I cannot get the horror out of my mind. I am destined to find the answer to the dream.

I have an idea! First, I steal a peek under my bed to see if he looks like he is smiling in his sleep. What benefit that is to me? I don't have a clue.

I did it. I actually felt like someone scared of heights standing on a nine-story ledge, peeking down for a look. What a dumb assed idea. My brother looked like a damned serial killer in his sleep too. Instantly, I got cold feet. So, I got one of my books from my drawer and read until that feeling subsided. It never subsided. Although that feeling never went away, I talk myself into waking the monster who was sleeping below me.

"Shawn, Shawn, Shaaawwwnnn" I say loud enough to be heard, but soft enough to calm the beast that may be awakened.

"What! What! What! You freakin' psycho!?" Shawn whispers at the top of his lungs. His eyes bulging out like a runaway slave.

"I had a dream." I return with a smile.

"OK, so you're Dr. Martin Luther King!" Shawn said no longer at a whisper. He continued to say, "Why do you always feel that you must get me up at the crack of dawn to tell me a freakin' dream, huh? Are you that sick? Are you that retarded? You don't think it could wait until the sun comes up?"

"I just want to tell you before I forget it, that's all."

"How can you forget that sick shit that is on your mind? It should be embedded in your mind forever! Or at least until breakfast."

"Well, I just thought…"

"Nope…I don't think that you did. Cause if you would have given it the slightest thought you would've let me sleep. Don't you think it could have waited until nine o'clock when I am fully awake? Of course it could have, but you have to have it your way and ruin my freakin' day. You just don't get it. You need a better shrink. You need to get your pills back. Every night you have these nightmares and you feel you need to share with them with the world…beginning with me. Like your dreams have some significance on other people's lives. Guess what! Reality check, we don't give a damned. For the past three months, I have felt the same way I felt today. I do not wanna hear this crap, because you give *me* nightmares! I tell mom, nothing happens, I tell dad, and it's even worse…He says, 'Shawn, that is your brother and if he has something he considers important to say to you should try to listen.' I try, believe me I try!" Shawn continues the tirade as he puts on his robe and helps me out of bed, where by the way, I was comfortable. "What about the times dad, I say…he wakes me up at five or six in the morning! This is a mental house…full of psychos! Mom, Dad, and you…especially you! And I have to be the one subjected to the Mental House Trilogies!"

"Well since you are awake…."

"Bite me!" Shawn said in a growl, as he pushes me out of our room and slams the door.

I walked down the hall in my underwear and into my parent's bedroom, pretending not to be bothered by his soliloquy.

"Mom, mom, moooom…" I began as with my brother.

"Yes dear."

"I had a dream."

"Whaddya thinking son…at this hour?" My father yawned in frustration as he looks at the clock by his bedside.

"Be quiet Eric, the boy's talking to me. What is it dear?" My mother retorts

"I had a dream. No mom, it was a nightmare! People were jumping out of a building, it was on fire!"

"Honey, did you know the people?" Mom asked concerned.

"Noooo!" I said excitedly. I was always one for overexcitement as it was part of my disease, so no one took me as seriously as I took myself. My mother responded in her known all too well condescending manner.

"I know honey, I know you're upset. But since we don't even know if these people exist, don't you think this revelation could wait until breakfast? Momma's gonna cook you something special when she gets up, and she is gonna hear all of your dreams," mom continued in third person as she spoke of herself. She did that a lot. I liked when she did. For some unknown reason it made me feel special, although I wished she would not do it in public. I felt I was too old for that kind of chatter. She would never talk to my brother in that tense, only me.

"OK, mom I will be back," I happily responded.

"Where are you going?" She demanded.

"Outside to play."

"Don't you think it's a little too early for that?"

"Jimmany Christmas, Tangie, let the boy go, so I can get a least a little rest before having to go to this freakin' driving class!" My father pleaded.

"Well, if you would not drink and drive, you would not have to attend the class."

"I was not drinking and driving, I just had one beer at the wrong time. And don't say that in front of the boy," my dad said sluggishly.

"If you were so concerned about shielding Roman, you wouldn't leave beer cans and empty half pints all over the house that takes an entire evening for me to clean up."

"I only do it because you enjoy it," my dad said without thinking, still buzzed from last night.

"Did you sleep with that whore because I enjoyed it?!"

"Son, it's ok for you to go outside if you want. Enjoy," my dad said in a sobered up tone.

I knew why my dad said it was ok. It was not because he wanted me to explore the world. It was because he did not want to hear my mom's wrath, nor any of my dreams. My dreams would tell of what was to be…good or bad. One nightmare, demanded special attention. It was what my mother referred to when she spoke of the affair. The dream did not occur every night, but rather on certain nights. The nights that my dad was working late, were strangely the nights that I experienced the dreams. Those nightmares became more and more frequent, as did his long hours. The dreams began the same way each time…dad driving a vehicle that was not our own. It was a newer looking ford model, mustang type, the convertible type that we could not afford. It was baby blue with chrome shoes, shining from bumper to bumper. The dream would begin with my dad driving the same route each time with a big smile on his face. The destination however changed from time to time. At times, my dad would drive to the station where he worked. Other times, he would drive to an undisclosed location; it appeared to be his co-worker's home. Then the dream would go down hill from there. My father would touch this woman, a woman that I have never seen before, in the way that he would touch mom. He then would grab her by the hair and pull her head back by the locks. Dad sucked on her bare neck, forced her down roughly, and peeled off her tight clothes. She was not bothered by my dad's roughness, as she giggled and returned the doffing. After seeing my father intimately entertain this woman, I woke up screaming. My dad would come into our room and try to console me. I did not want him to touch me. I felt bad for rejecting him. I kept telling myself it was just a dream. Although I knew it was not just a dream, because it felt so real that my mind would not let go. This dream reoccurred in my sleep for weeks. At first, I never told anyone the content of the dreams…not the psychologist, not my mom, not even Shawn, who would usually tolerate my dreams as long as I found the right time to express them. The dream became more graphic and revealing as time passed. I just wished it would go away; but it would not. I eventually had to break the silence, in order to save my dad's life.

The last nightmare I had the horror of dreaming, changed our lives. The dream began as it always did…my dad driving somewhere in a mustang we could not afford. The destination was at his station. Again, my dad walked into work, made small talk with his fellow comrades, and the woman I did not know. Someone at his job said her name in conversation…it was Ms. Clara! My dad stayed late that evening with Ms. Clara while the rest of the team retired for the day. And again, rather graphically he made love to Ms. Clara. When they finished doing their business, he offered Ms. Clara a ride home *in her own mustang.* The destination was the same place that I saw them make love for the first time. They never reached the destination. My dad was in a traumatic car accident with this woman. The accident had placed him in critical condition in the intensive care unit and it killed Ms. Clara. When I awoke, my vision was blurry from crying in my sleep. My dad had just left for work.

My mom asked me why I was so upset. I told her. I told her about the accident, that was the part that frightened me. She stopped me, and started to guide me exactly to the particular points in the dream that she wanted to hear. When I finished telling her the vision, we went directly to the station and waited by the car. Like clockwork, as in all of my dreams, the truth was revealed. My dad and this home wrecker, as my mom would refer to her as, were taking their drunken gait towards the baby blue mustang. They were laughing and touching—oblivious to the fact that my mom was in the area, watching their every move. As they got closer they were met my mom's fury and me. The look that my mom gave them made Ms. Clara sober up at once. A streak of trepidation ran through her. A streak that changed her loud giggle into a terrified aphonia, and made her lose control of her bowels. The smile on my dad's face turned into a sick embarrassing look that I unfortunately understood all too well. My mother did also, and marched directly to him and let him have it. She slapped the fire out of him.

"What in the hell are you doing with that pissy tailed bitch?!" My mom blared. She then assumed a fighting stance just in case my father was to return the favor. He did not.

Clara just walked away quickly as if she was never walking with my dad. She possessed a fear that was beyond explanation.

"I am so sorry Tangie. I am very embarrassed by my behavior…and I hope to God that you can forgive me," dad said apologetically, with a tear in his eye. It was unclear if the tear was from the slap or from the embarrassment. My guess was the slap. It hurt me. Wherever it was from, it was real. It was so real that my mom lost all of her fire. It transformed into sadness. She was mad at herself for losing that spark, because she wanted to kick his ass good. She had already called her brothers to meet us at the condo. She put her head down and shook it in disbelief. She said nothing to him. When mom finally looked up, she searched for a glimpse of Ms. Clara. Ms. Clara took the mustang and was long gone. I was glad that Ms. Clara had left, because the way mom hit dad, Ms. Clara would have really been hurt. Although I did not like her, I did not want to see her catch a fresh one like that. Mom and I walked home alone. I knew my mom was angry, because she hit dad. She hit dad so hard her fingerprints were embedded in his face. I never saw her hit dad. Her eyes were blood red from crying so much, but she would wipe the tears before she thought that I could see them. I saw them though, and hugged her in hopes that she would've felt better.

Later that following week when my mom was ready to talk to my dad, she told him the entire story, starting with the dreams I had expressed.

"I don't believe that Tangela. Honestly, I think you were following me," dad said calmly and quietly.

"If I knew you were a freakin' cheater, I would have, just so I would not have had to take my son with me...I would have really busted some ass then!" My mom yelled loud enough for the neighbors to hear.

My dad got this chill. He knew it had to be true. My mom would never have brought me if she intended on fighting. She had more respect for us than that.

Mom never really looked at dad in the same way again. She was thankful that I saved his life, even if it exposed his infidelity. Dad slept on the couch for months after that incident. And as far as I knew, he never slept with Ms. Clara again.

Chapter II

The auditorium at Public School 13…

"…and the home of the Braaaave!" In the auditorium, the students recited the pledge of allegiance and clamored through the national anthem in a key unknown to Francis Scott.

"Announcements will be shared by Ms. Adaire," Principal Reed said. Students quietly took their seats as she walked on the stage. Although she was a dean for the school, we respected Ms. Adaire like she was the assistant principal of PS 13.

"Good morning Principal Reed, members of the faculty, and my beloved students," Ms. Adaire said without emotion.

"I am here to speak about three things that are of importance. 1. There is a criminal in this school. You may call him or her a graffiti artist. I will say this plainly. There is no art in vandalism. Listen to me each one of you. I am not happy about this writing on the walls or in the bathrooms. If you know who is causing your school to look like a ghetto, let me know." Someone was overheard saying, "be a snitch." Ms. Adaire continued as if she did not hear them, "You will not be considered a snitch, on the contrary, we will be very proud of you for helping us keep your school safe and clean. Also, no one will ever know that you said anything. It will be kept confidential. Those of you who are destroying our schools, you will be caught. And when you are caught, you will get just what you deserve. I will make you that promise.

2. The disrespect of the faculty and staff will not be tolerated. I do not care if you are talking to the maintenance person or the principal, you better know how

to address them. Two individuals were suspended last week for being disrespect-ful to a teacher. If you are looking for a free ticket to stay home with your parents and probably not passing to the next grade, then act like those two suspended individuals. If you want to graduate and do greater things, then attend class, do the work, and stop being a menace.

3. I am developing a…" as she was speaking, David, a student in the audito-rium made the mistake of whispering to his friend, Danielle. Ms. Adaire paused for a moment then focused her attention on the disobedient boy, "David, don't just tell Danielle. Why don't you tell the entire auditorium what's so important. Oh, *it must be important* because you have interrupted the announcements and you have interrupted *me*. Is what you have to say that important…IS IT?"

David nods his head negatively in trepidation.

"I did not think so…I suggest that when you hear me speaking, you listen and not talk!" She glared at him for about five seconds after the tirade. David sank into the auditorium chair like melted caramel. The auditorium was quiet. Ms. Adaire's breathing pattern was the only sound audible.

Ms. Adaire cleared her throat; not only to remove the foreign object from the lungs, but also to ascertain compliance with her demand for silence.

She continued, this time with tenderness in her voice, "Our school has been invited to participate in a city-wide chess tournament. I was asked to coach a team of chess players. I need to know how many of our students enjoy playing chess, or at the very least are interested in learning. Raise your hands if you are interested in playing chess." Many hands went up. "Keep your hands up until you receive a permission slip from your teacher." Those having raised their hands were all provided permission slips to have signed by their parents.

Approximately thirty students attended the first week of practice. The atten-dance dwindled to about five after the next three weeks. Among these five, Nicky and I had been the best among them.

A young boy cursed by a spirit of death and destruction, Nicky was called to Ms. Adaire's office a few times. He was never suspended. It was not that his offenses could not warrant suspension. Anything could warrant suspension under Ms. Adaire's discipline. Ms. Adaire knew he was struggling in life, so she spent more time counseling Nicky than she did punishing him.

Nicky was one of the first to have his permission slip signed and returned to Ms. Adaire. When Ms. Adaire found out that Nicky wanted to play, she sent a pass to his teacher requesting he come to her office. He knew where her office was by heart. Nicky walked down the long hallway to her office the same way, he always did when he was in trouble. Down the main corridor, one hand in the pocket, with a be-bop strut. When little Nicky arrived, she sat him down and began to question him.

"Nicky, how many times have you been in my office for disciplinary action?"

"I think two times Ms. Adaire," Nicky said nervously. As Ms. Adaire was looking for his discipline record in her files, Nicky blurted out, "Ms. Adaire I'm not the one who wrote on the walls…it was Eric. I knew he was doing something wrong, so I did not even use the bathroom, I just went back to the classroom."

Ms. Adaire, pretending to ignore Nicky's confession, found his files, and placed them on her desk. She reviewed them for a moment, while he sat nervously in silence.

"Nicky, you have been in my office five times since the first day of class. That is a bit excessive. What is going on?" Ms. Adaire inquired.

"I dunno."

"Nicky, I know you did not vandalize the school…that is not why you're here. I just want to talk with you for a while. Is that ok?"

"Sure."

"Nicky, your teacher seems to think that you are very smart. She wants to recommend you for e-track, but your behavior is keeping you from attaining that privilege," she said in a caring manner. Nicky did not say anything. "Nicky, would you like to be considered for e-track?" Ms. Adaire asked as she chipped through his icy coldness with her eyes. Nicky shrugged his shoulders as he made eye contact with the floor.

"Look at me Nicky," she said firmly in order to get his attention. "I also think that you have potential. If I thought you were just some punk kid and didn't care, I would not waste my time talking to you. I would just suspend you and be done with it. I do suspend students you know. Now I am not going to sit here and tell you I like to do it. But what I will tell you is that *I will do it.* If it is what needs to be done. I prefer to talk to my students, allow them the opportunity to listen, and hopefully they will change. Do you understand what I am saying Nicky?" Nicky *overstood* what Ms. Adaire was saying. Knowing that she was trying her best reach him, he opened up a bit.

"What does your mom do for a living Nicky?" She brings her chair around towards him so that they are no longer separated by the desk.

"She takes care of my brothers and sister."

"How many brothers and sisters do you have?"

"One sister and three brothers."

"Does your dad work?"

"Yes."

"What does he do?"

"He hustles."

"He hustles? What do you mean by that?"

"I don't really know, that's what my dad says he does. He goes out at night and brings my mom home some money...but my mom says that he needs another hustle because that one ain't payin' the bills." Ms. Adaire saw more than what was said and wanted to laugh, but she just smiled. Nicky seemed to have read Ms. Adaire's expression and let out a smile that undoubtedly helped break the ice.

"I see...do your parents argue a lot?"

"No, not really," Nicky answered. After another pause, this time not so awkward, Ms. Adaire asked, "Can you play chess, Nicky? Or are you joining the team because you want to learn?"

"Oh, I can play really well. I play on my computer all the time. Sometimes I play with my dad, when he has the time. My brothers and sisters play too. I can beat my brother, and he is two years older than me!" Nicky said enthusiastically.

"I was thinking if I should even allow you to play on the team. I have seen you in my in my office too many times since school began," she said now breaking eye contact with him to stare out of the window.

"Ms. Adaire, if you let me play...I won't get in trouble. I promise. I want to be on the team."

"Okay then, let's make a deal. I do not want to see you in my office for any disciplinary actions the entire time you are on my team. If I do, then we will have to rethink your position on this team. Do you get what I am saying to you?"

"I get it."

"Good. Make me proud that I allowed you to participate on the chess team."

"I will Ms. Adaire!"

"You can return to your classroom. And tell Mrs. Lee to call me."

"I will Ms. Adaire," Nicky responded as he ran back to his classroom.

A few minutes later, the phone in Ms. Adaire's office rings.

"Hello, public school 13, Ms. Adaire, how may I help you?"

"Ms. Adaire you asked me to call you?" Mrs. Lee inquired.

"Yes, send Eric to my office."

Danny was an intellectual juggernaut who did not have many friends. He actually improved his social skills by being on the team. He didn't care for the game much, but did enjoy the attention he received from the team. The team focused on his attributes, not his disabilities. Danny was bright, and he knew how to strategize. He was also obese, he knew how to eat. Ms. Adaire would never allow anyone to make fun of Danny's weight. After awhile, it wasn't even important.

Erika and Derika were identical twins. Although they both loved every aspect of the game, they were not very skilled. They played every day together and even bought books of instruction by the chess greats. They were not allowed to go to the park and play, their parents would not allow it. Their father was a famous musician, and sheltered them from the real world. He forbade them from entertaining strangers. Consequently, the only way they could strengthen their game was to play at practice.

Nicky played chess well. Ms. Adaire allowed him to be on the team as long as she did not have to see him in her office. He agreed. Although he was not in Ms. Adaire's homeroom class, he joined our class for special events. He liked coming to our class, even though Ms. Adaire was mean, and yelled a lot.

He and I were rivals during practice. Before practice started, we would take out our own board and play until the team came. Ms. Adaire would have to split us up so that the team would be stronger.

Our team had been practicing for months, and we were ready. The tournament was next month. Even Ms. Adaire was proud of the team's progress. The last practice before the game, Ms. Adaire walked into the classroom with a huge box. Everyone wondered what was in the box. She would not tell us until the end of practice. As we played, we guessed of all kinds of things we thought might be in the box. Books to study, maybe new clocks, we even asked Ms. Adaire to give us a hint. She stood her ground and made us wait until the end of practice. Five minutes before the end of practice, she revealed the mystery of the box.

"I took the liberty of purchasing the team chess uniforms. The pants may have to be tailored, but the shirts should fit. You will receive three shirts that have your first names embossed on them, one pair of black pants, and a note of correspondence for your parents. The blue shirt is for you to wear wherever you like, the black and white shirts are for competition. Do not wear shirts that are for competition. I will tell you which color shirt we will be wearing for each competition. The letter is not for you, ***SO DO NOT OPEN IT!***" Ms. Adaire said in her dean's voice. The same voice we thought was not allowed in the chess practices.

Danny was the first to pick up his uniform. His had to be husky, because Danny was a big boy. He smiled and showed the shirt for all to see. This made us all the more eager to receive our uniforms.

Erika and Derika were next. Their uniforms were as skinny as they were. They were the tallest players on our team, but there was no meat on the bones. They were always dressed in the latest fashions and always had money in their pockets. We thought they were rich and stuck up, but when we started playing chess together, we saw the cool side of them.

Nicky, with his famous walk, strolls up to the box. He does the same strut with minor variations to whatever the situation. If he's in trouble…it's the one-hand in the pocket strut. If he's getting an award, it's the two-handed strut. Or even if he is going to the bathroom…it's the hand on the pelvis strut. In his mind, he was the shiznit.

Then there was me. The freakin' weirdo. I thought everyone was looking at me as I walked to her desk. Ms. Adaire had the uniforms waiting for me. I started to feel the pressure overcome me. I had to grab the uniforms with both hands. That was not enough. Then I had to put them to my face and smell them. I wish that was enough, but it wasn't. I had to then touch Ms. Adaire's other hand. I just pretended I was shaking her hand and saying thank you. Mrs. Adaire was aware of my anxiety all along. She just politely said as she winked at me, "I appreciate your gratitude, but people in The United States normally shake with the right hand." She then shook my left hand with hers. I wondered if she knew that I had OCD.

The team sat around after practice to play and show off our uniforms with our names on them. We talked about how we felt about each other in the beginning. One of the things we said was that we thought the twins were stuck up…Erika and Derika thought I was crazy…Danny thought Nicky was not smart because he wasn't in the e-track…and we all thought Danny was a bully that would eat anyone who went close to him. We laughed at the misconceptions that we had about each other. Although we were different, we no longer felt different. At this moment, we really felt like a team.

Ms. Adaire would always drill in us little clichés that we would use in competition. Like the one she would lead us into after practice was over, "What's more important winning or losing?" Our response was, "Having a good time, because we're already winners." Or she would say, "Good Offense…" we would respond, "Wins games!" She would then say, "Good Defense…" we would respond, "Wins championships!" She enjoyed those little sayings. We would say them in every practice. She would also add another principle every week. She ran a very tight ship. Although she was stern, we had a lot of fun together.

Chapter III

I waited for the elevator for about five minutes. Five minutes to me was like five hours. As I waited, people were just bypassing the elevator and taking the steps. I wondered if the elevator was out of service. When the pigeon lady pushing her shopping cart went into the staircase, I said to myself this is ridiculous. If she could walk up the steps, shopping cart, stale bread and all, then I could also. I am not going to wait here all day. I was hungry. I left the elevator, and took the steps. I began at a quick pace. That lasted for about three flights. After reaching the sixth floor my legs started to give. I was pissed at my legs for betraying me; they gave out at the worst possible time. My brother's friends were on the next flight of steps, "lighting it up". My legs giving out, not to mention all of the contact I was about to catch from these assholes exasperated me. When they saw me coming up the stairs, they blew smoke in my face. I tried to hold my breath, but after thirty seconds of direct blows from the chronic, I was knocked down. I quickly returned to my feet and tried to dance around the delinquents, but they held me there and continued to blow smoke in my face. Then I tried the rope a dope. This seemed to work. They let me pass, but by that time, they had the stairwell so foggy, I felt like I was walking on clouds. By the time I reached the ninth floor, I knew that I was. I felt like a rock star.

As I walked down the hallway, coming closer to my apartment, the odor of spinach transformed into the odor of collared greens. As I entered the house, I saw my mom and gave her a big hug. She was warm and sweaty. My mom was getting busy in the kitchen. As my aunt would say, she put her foot in it. I recently learned that it meant she cooked the dish well, not that she actually put her foot in the food. Whatever she was cooking, it smelled delicious. My mom took pride in being able to cook anything edible. If it were once living, she could make it worth the killing.

I walked over to my mom, gave her the sealed envelope from Ms. Adaire, and got some cookies to hold me until dinner as she read the letter silently. She got through the first pages ok, but when she got to the third and thereafter, she just broke down. She could not stop the tears from streaming down her face. I asked her what was wrong, but she just waived me away. I went upstairs and told my brother that mom was crying. My brother, being zooted, and having the munchies, just took the cookies out of my hand and ate them. I just left him alone, because I knew he was bent. I went to dad's room and told him that mom was crying. When dad and I went down stairs, my brother was staggering behind us. By the time we got to the kitchen, she had stopped crying. She told my dad that nothing was wrong. She said that she just got sentimental. She slipped him the letter. He placed it in his pocket without reading it. He went upstairs to read the letter in privacy.

My brother just looked at me as if to say, freakin weirdo, and he made me feel all the better. I forgot about why my mom had been crying and I started smiling. I know he wanted to get at me. However, with mom being right there, and Shawn being high, he decided to make an exit.

I put on my favorite shirt, the blue shirt that let everyone know I was a member of public school thirteen's chess team. I slid on a pair of jeans, and walked outside into the cool air.

"Nino, que pasa?" Mrs. Mayra said as I walked past the benches in front of the building.

"Hi, Mrs. Mayra," I responded. I sat down for a minute or two and chatted with her. She always enjoyed my company. Although I did not realize it at the time, she was teaching me Spanish and I was teaching her English.

"A donde va?"

"Huh?"

"Where you go now?" Mrs. Mayra inquired.

"Oh, no say…I am just walking," I responded with the little Spanish she had taught me.

"Boy, yo mama let you go outside without no coat on?" Mr. Joe interrupted.

"Hi, Mr. Joe…I didn't think it was frio outside."

"Free…ain't nothing free in this world son, you better stay in school and let Mrs. Adaire teach you somethin'."

I chalked it up to Mr. Joe's hearing aid. He had trouble hearing since he was in Nam. Mr. Keaton, (Nicky's grandfather and Mr. Joe's best friend) made it back from the war, but they were never the same. Mr. Nicky had mental problems. We called him the crazy man, because he talked to himself a lot. Although Mr. Joe was not affected mentally, he has metal in his back and in his legs from being wounded in war. He said it was "shrapnel". He used to visit Mr. Keaton when he was admitted to the psychiatric ward. If you talk to Mr. Joe about the wars, all he says is he's glad he returned home, because a lot of his brothers were killed or missing in action. He never talks about the people he killed. When I asked, he would say to me, "boy don't you have something better to do in life than talk about death?" I guess that is why I have patience for Mr. Joe, he has lived a hard life. I don't think he is as mean on the inside as he pretends to be.

The air tasted like autumn, not just on my tongue, but also on my frenulum, on the cilia of my nares, on my conjunctiva and everywhere I believed a receptor could receive the stimulus. The blades of fresh cut grass, the pine scent emanating from the mighty perennials. The pasty odor of the city pigeons trying to hustle the same old lady out of her bag of stale bread.

The atmosphere attempted to hoodwink the hood into believing that the country was close, however I knew that it was not. As I looked above me, the project buildings stood like evergreens. This was my proof. I never saw the projects in the country.

I wandered about in a daze; partly from the contact that I received and partly from the dreams, not really knowing what to do to clear my mind. I skipped into the subway station, not to travel, but just to walk around. As I jumped the turnstile, I was taken back to see the number of homeless just walking around the station.

There was one woman in particular that caught everyone's eye. She appeared about thirty-one years of age, moderately overweight, and severely disheveled. She was clearly schizophrenic. I continued down the steps peeking at this woman, trying not to stare too hard because I did not want to arouse her curiosity. She walked about the platform talking to herself in an angry tone, and harassed the individuals trying to get to work on time. She followed behind them, and mimicked them. Although she sported an entire winter outfit, she would touch their clothing, as if she had just discovered that people wore clothes. She saw me ogling. I could not help it. The things she was doing made her appear to be a bit unbalanced. I say that euphemistically. I broke contact with her for a second or two. It worked. She resumed her antagonistic ways. There was a man sprawled out on the bench where you wait for your train to enter the tracks. He slept in the station so sound that he was drooling and snoring at the same time. No one else was able to rest due to him hogging all the seats. When the homeless woman approached him, she tried to wake him up. She shook his shoulders, even slapped his face. When all of those tactics failed, she then pulled out one of her sloppy breasts and put it on his drooling lips. *OH MY GOD!* I remember thinking to myself. At this point, I lost all voluntary muscle control of my eyes and neck. I could not turn my face from this lady's antics. I guess she felt she was giving him payment for the bottled water she had confiscated. She opened the bottle of water, and walked off. The man never awoke from his drunken stupor. Instead of drinking the bottled water, she began pouring the water atop of her head as if she were outside in the desert. The temperature was only about fifty degrees outside and it really didn't change much when you entered the station.

The New York Police Department began to assemble themselves in her vicinity. There were enough officers to allow a presence to be felt, but not enough to be threatening in any way. The police did not want to get her riled up. The stench was atrocious. The officers called for backup. The backup came immediately, but that did not change the situation. No officer wanted to be the first to approach her. Who wanted to tussle with that stankness? The only guarantee the police had at this time was that she wasn't afraid to give them a tussle. She was like a wild animal; nothing seemed to tame her. If anyone caused a threat, aroused her curiosity, or even intimately focused on each other, she responded. She responded like a wild beast. No one in the subway...not the individuals going to work, nor the other homeless who in fact were just as crazy as she was, not even the police who were sworn to protect, wanted any parts of her.

I thought for a split second that I was still dreaming. I knew I wasn't when she caught me gawking a second time. Immediately I broke eye contact, but this time it did not work. I aroused her curiosity. She began coming towards me as if she wanted to offer me something in return for something that I may have had. I did not know what it was she had to offer, nor did I care to find out. As she approached with her jagged gait, I retreated backward slowly up the stairs. She started to pick up pace. I turned around and began to walk-run. This pace did not help keep distance between us; therefore, I began to jog. She began to jog behind me. I ran like hell. I ran faster than I ever ran before. I ran like my life depended on it. I ran right past the nervous police officers. As I ran, I began to think. If she could perform her capers with the police officers on post, what would she do if she got a hold to me? Those thoughts commanded my feet to keep distance between us. I sprung up the first set of stairs, innately touching both sides of the railing. I burst through the turnstile, onto the second set of steps, out of the station, and onto the sidewalk. The organ inside my chest was playing the house version of heartbeat. I looked back to see if she was still behind me, she was not. That entire episode made me wonder what I must have done to displease the gods. I continued to walk, my heart rate started to settle down. I knew because I felt the entropy. It was still difficult for me to breathe, but after a while, the feeling subsided.

I crossed the street and saw Mr. James coming out of his bar. Mr. James was one of the Tuskegee Airmen. Although he was too young at the time to pilot an aircraft in the war, he had pictures taken of him and the original Tuskegee Airmen who did pilot aircraft. Mr. James had a strong lisp, when he relaxed his tongue. Although Mr. James was twice my dad's age, he and my dad appeared to be good friends. My dad being a functioning alcoholic, made friends with anyone who owned such an establishment. Mr. James was cleaning up his bar after a long night of partying, he walked outside for some fresh air at the same time that I was crossing the street.

"Come on in an' shit fo a minute." Mr. James rolled off his tongue as if he had said it correctly all along.

I looked at him strangely for about a half of second, just enough time for me to interpret the true meaning behind his lisp.

"Oh, uh, hi, Mr. James," I said as I walked right into his lounge. I remembered my dad taking my brother and me to his lounge to get a burger. Mr. James made the best burgers in town. We ate while my dad went to the bar to chat with Mr. James, or so he said. When we left Mr. James' lounge, Mr. James and my dad had the same lisp. My brother and I already knew that my dad was placing bets with Mr. James. Mr. James also ran numbers out of his lounge. Every now and then, my dad would hit the number and take my mom out to some place fancy. I would have to stay home with Shawn, who soon after they left, would have a house party.

After nine o'clock, Mr. James' lounge totally changed. The music became that old music that my dad played around the house when he got a little tipsy. The crowd also took on another face. The median age increased, and the older people came in dressed like they were going to church.

I glanced at the chessboard that was on the table, as I always did when dad took us here to eat.

"You know how to play chess, don't cha?" asked Mr. James rhetorically.

"Yes sir, but how did you know?" I responded

"I could tell by the way you were thinkin' out loud, looked like you were pon-derin' a chess move…oh and by the way I like the shirt."

Instantly, I felt ridiculous. I forgot that I had my chess team shirt on. I am also sure that my dad told him that my brother and I were on chess teams, he enjoyed bragging about us.

"So you wanna teash me som'um or what?" Mr. James said in a southern accent.

"Uh…Okay," I said as I sat at the table. I honestly didn't feel like playing with Mr. James. I had something else on my mind. It was the dreams.

"Looks like somthins' on yur mind. Let me buy you a drink, and you can get it off your chest," Mr. James said with a smile.

"You know I can't drink," I said condescendingly.

"Well how on Earth will you survive?" Mr. James let out a hearty laugh, as he directed me to the bar.

"How about a virgin screwdriver rocked out leaning to the shyde pimpin?" said Mr. James.

"Huh?" I said as I looked at him strangely. I really had a hard time under-standing him. I not only had to overcome the lisp, but the ancient slang he used sounded like the King James Version of the Holy Bible.

"Transhlation, Orange Juice with ice with a skraw honey," his wife said post-drunkenly as she slid on a robe to hide the obvious fact that she was in Vic-toria's Lingerie. She began to finish cleaning up where he had left off. She was attractive and appeared to be markedly younger than the age of Mr. James.

"I will also get you something to eat if you're hungry," She said with a south-ern type of hospitality.

I forgot all about what my mom had told me about breakfast. I asked, "Mr. James can I have a burger? I can pay for it."

"Nonsense, today you are our guest," Mrs. James said.

"Now, I am gonna to put your burger on, and you just sit back and eat it. Okay?" Mrs. James responded rhetorically.

"Delilah honey, put a burger on for little Eric," Mr. James said as if he didn't hear our conversation. He had no idea what my name was, he just knew my brother and I were my father's sons, so he would just call us both little Eric's. I didn't correct him; I actually kinda liked it. I just pretended as if it were my name.

"Why are you out so early anyways, walking about the skreet like dis'?" he asked.

My heart lit up when he asked me this, because I knew that he genuinely wanted to know the answer to his question. I could not get the response out of my mouth fast enough. Forgetting all that happened to me at the train station, I began to speak of my dreams.

"I had one dream after another. They were crazy!" I said in excitement.

"Maybe you could sell your dreams and call them...call them..." He thought for a minute and at the same time we said, "*The Roman Opening.*" We both paused. It was bizarre. How could he and I be on the same page with the name of *my* chronicle of dreams? It made no sense. Oh, but it did....it made a lot of sense. I began to take him on a journey...We began to travel through my mind...

Chapter IV

The day of the tournament…

"Roman, save your knights for the family forks that I showed you. It will shut them down, I guarantee it!" Shawn said confidently.

"Mom, did Ms. Adaire tell you what shirt we're wearing?"

"Yes honey, wear the white one," she replied.

"You must be going away to play," Shawn chimed in.

"Yeah, we're gonna go to PS 86 in Jamaica, Queens."

"Roman, did you take your medication?"

"No mom, I skipped meds for the past two days. They make me tired, and I want to be able to think clearly," I said. Mom did not say anything. Instead, she went upstairs and came down with a garment bag and a large gift.

"Mom, what's in the box?" I inquired.

"Something that the parents decided to get for Ms. Adaire, since she has been an inspiration to you kids."

We met up with the team at the competition floor. Everyone was there waiting on us. We exchanged greetings. Ms. Adaire and the parents exchanged hugs and kisses.

"Danny, I have got to show you this new move," I said.

"Erika showed me a move in her book that I think I am gonna try," Danny replied.

"You can show it to me Roman," Derika said.

"I'll show it to you if you tell LaShawn that I am cool," I answered.

"You like LaShawn, huh? Ok. I will think about it." They both started to smile as he pulled out his chessboard.

"No chessboards out. We do not want them to see our styles just yet. Put them back in your bags until we are in our thinking rooms," Ms. Adaire reminded us.

"We will be adhering to the official rules of the World Chess Federation. This will be a double elimination bout. If you are disqualified for unsportsmanlike conduct, this will be counted as a double disqualification. There are five school teams participating today. These school teams are PS.13 The Strategists; PS 206 The Jousters; PS 24 The Thinkers; PS 61 The Hawks; and the hosting team, PS 86 The Dungeon Masters," the official reported to the teams participating.

The hosting team PS 86, The Dungeon Masters, was the team to beat. Everyone knew them for being the strongest team in the competition. They also had a lady coach. They called her the "Queen Bee." She wasn't a teacher though. She worked in the library. Actually, disguised as a librarian, she played chess most of the time. We were nervous, but after listening to Ms. Adaire's pep talk, we felt like there was nothing that we could not accomplish.

"Listen guys we got em'. We are the Strategists; we can out think the jousters. The thinkers, all they can do is think. We will strategize and blow right past them…and the hawks, have you ever seen a bird that played a board game? The Dungeon Masters think they have an advantage because we are in their house, but let me tell you something, that was their worst mistake. When we finish with them, they'll be begging to get out of their own dungeon. Now if you won't do it for yourselves, do it for me, because I want it…understand me? Let's bring home something to show our school that we at least practiced. By the way, what is the most important thing? Winning or losing?"

"Having a good time because we are already winners!" We all said in unison. It was something that she instilled in us the first day we began practicing. She knew then that we were ready for our first match. "Are we ready? On three Strategists…ready?! One! Two! Three!"

We all responded Strategists as if we were thirty players deep.

We went in the auditorium that day knowing that we were winners, even if we did not win one game.

We began with Danny playing someone from the hawks. Danny dusted the guy off. Erika played someone from the Dungeon Masters and got dusted off. Derika played someone on the thinkers and barely got a win. Nicky played a girl from the jousters. This chick gave Nicky a hard time. It was the best game yet. That set the tone for our concentration. Nicky finally won, but it took a toll on his mental stamina. Nicky's mom, Mrs. Keaton, who Ms. Adaire and the parents intimately nicknamed Kay Kay, was so proud of Nicky. She had no idea her son was so good at chess.

Nicky had to take a break. Ms. Adaire put Erika and me in again. It was sudden death for Erika, because if she lost this time, there was no placement for her, this made her focus intensely. She played against another Jouster that had already lost one game. She beat him. And she beat him well. Her moves were executed perfectly. The guy didn't even wait for checkmate; he resigned. She was soo excited she jumped up and gave Ms. Adaire a hug that almost broke her back. Ms Adaire was excited also, but tried to curb the enthusiasm. "Good job Erika, but you need to stay focused…it becomes more challenging the higher you advance." "Okay Ms. Adaire," she said as she smiled proudly, although much of what she heard was muffled by the *good jobs* she continued to receive. Her parents looked on, but could not speak from the ropes. Unless you were an official or a coach, it had to be quiet in the arena.

"Good Job Erika," Roman whispered.

We continued to play. The finalists in the competition were the Dungeon Masters and us, The Strategists. I was the only one who did not have any losses, and a guy name Tye, from PS 86. We were in the bracket to play against one another in the finals. I had already clinched an individual bronze for the school. We also won the certificate for the team with the highest team score. It was time to play the last two games. This was for the silver and the gold. If I could only hang in there for two more games. The first game for the silver, I beat Corey. The last game I had to play Tye. Ms. Adaire was just as excited as the twins at this point. She was warned to settle down, or we would be docked a point. Ms. Adaire regained her composure. In the final game, we had to choose the piece.

"What difference does it make?" Tye asked.

"The white piece has nine tenth of a percent advantage over the black pieces," Danny responded out of turn. Ms Adair gave a look to all of us with her finger to her lips as to say, be very quiet, this is important.

The pieces seemed to move themselves, as I just touched the clock. A strange feeling came over me. I felt as if I had to touch the clock again, but it was not my move. I did it. I touched the clock.

"Dude, you can't stop the clock on my turn!" Tye whispered as he gave me a warning. Something was burning inside of me. I had to touch it one more time. I was distracted. It was hard for me to think. I remembered what my brother said about the knights, so I brought them out. He did not seem to be effected by them. As soon as I got them in striking range and he pushed pawn to threaten. It worked. I backed up and lost the initiative. He then took the knight with a discovery. I began to counterattack with a dragon tail. I moved and touched the clock. The feeling returned.

"Mom, something weird is going on with Romie. I can see it in his face," Shawn whispered in a concerned voice. She acknowledged, but did not respond. Still looking intensely at the game.

Romie, do not touch that clock again. Shawn thought to himself. I went for the clock a third time, Tye pushed pawn and touched it first, although he was very irritated, because he wasn't finished thinking. I kept my composure well until the middle game. That was as far as my restraint would hold. Without my medication, I went berserk. I began pressing the clock, I pressed it about six times...three with each hand. The official could not overlook this crazy behavior. I was disqualified. I quietly got up and walked directly to my team's table, where Ms. Adaire was waiting with a big smile.

"You did a great job and we are all proud of you!" Ms. Adaire said as she looked to the team for support.

"Yeah, you did great," everyone chimed in.

What made you hit the clock so many times dude? You had him on the ropes," Nicky said after saying I did great, negating his first response. It seemed like the entire team was looking for that answer, but I did not have one to give them. Ms. Adaire did.

"What is the most important thing...winning or losing?"

"Having a good time because we are already winners," we said in unison as we had been drilled to say.

"Correct! Now let's go out there, shake hands, and make new friends." I began shaking everyone's hand twice, with each hand. The judges were looking at me. I just knew they thought I was a weirdo. The other players thought it was cool and began copying me.

The judges collaborated in their booths. After discussing the results, they announced the scores and the winners.

We took second place overall. The Dungeon Masters came in first place. We received the individual honorable mention for most improved player, which was won by Erika. Everyone took home a certificate and a trophy for participation. I took home the silver medal for individual player wins. I even won an award for sportsmanship. I guess they thought I was shaking hands like that to be a good sportsman. I accepted. Tye and Corey took Gold and Bronze respectively.

As we were about to leave Kay asked Ms. Adaire to stay for a moment.

"Ms. Adaire, you can't leave yet honey, the moms want to take the winning coach out to dinner," Kay said.

"But, we didn't win Kay, we came in second," Ms. Adaire whispered as if the parents misunderstood the results and to hide the embarrassment.

"What's more important? Winning or Losing?" Tangie whispered in return. We all began to laugh. Most of the father's did not make it to the competition. The one dad that had come, Danny's father, felt no obligation to go to the after party with a bunch of women. He left his wife with some pocket money and went home to watch the game. The mothers took us to *The Outback Steakhouse*. Just as they were about to order, Tangie pulled out the gift and said a few words on behalf of the parents.

"Ms. Adaire, on behalf of all of the parents we would like to say that we love you, and want to thank you for what you have done for our children. Not only have our children been provided with the best teacher NYC has to offer, we have obtained a great chess coach, a great leader, and a role model. Our children look up to you Ms. Adaire, and so do we. So we put our money together and brought you something, so that you can always remember your favorite team. Go ahead, open it."

When she opened the gift, she was shocked. It was a marble chess set with a brass plate with everyone's name engraved on it. It also read Coach Claire Adaire, Thanks for making us number one *The Strategists*. It also had a photo album of all of the practices and tournament play. The first picture was Ms. Adaire and the entire team in their uniforms. Ms. Adaire cried.

"Okay, okay, enough of all of that. It's time to eat let's get down to business and don't be shy, because Jennifer's paying," Kay said.

Jennifer, the mother of the twins pulled out her gold card and said, "Thanks Kay, if it weren't for you, I wouldn't know what a gold card was for. Let the festivities begin!"

We sat at a table in the corner, not too far from our parents. We were in eyesight, but not in earshot. This was how we liked it, and obviously how they wanted it. We knew because as soon as we sat down, they were gone. I was saving a seat for my mom. When I had looked around, she had already posted up at another table with Ms. Adaire. Whatever they were talking about, Ms. Adaire sure was enjoying it. Ms. Adaire had a smile on her face that I had never seen before. It was not the cordial smile she gives to the parents on parent teacher night, nor was it the phony smile given to the principal as he took the podium. It was a different kind of smile, for the first time, Ms. Adaire looked pretty.

When I got home that evening, I began a serious cleansing ritual. I touched things around the house with both of my hands in a series of two...two for second place. I went upstairs and continued the ritual in my room. After touching my pillow in a series of two, I went to sleep. A spirit disturbed my rest...

Chapter V

Corey Speaks….

How did I get here? I ask myself, having played the endgame repeatedly in my mind. Ninety-nine percent of the chess players will never be invited. Of the few that *are invited*, most will decline the offer. Whether it was a lack of courage or a supreme state of intelligence, some were able to stand fast in the midst of seduction. That particular checkmate pattern had played out many times before, but how the pattern was introduced, in itself was surreal. I felt a sickness in my stomach when the tide had turned, I was one move away from sudden death, and I did it. I summoned the beast…

To many, chess is a boring game. To the few, a very special few, it is the only true game of the mind and the soul that still exists. A grandmaster had to be invited to see the games played out. The game was only played once. If you were not privileged to observe, you would never see it. Only invited grandmasters were allowed to enter into the ring. It was a state of mind. You joined with a concerted effort of mental power. The chess games were never recorded. There was no way to record them. No paper. No pen. No mind. The only mind that could record the games were the minds that were playing. That did not matter and you will understand why as we enter into the arena. This is my version…

After school at Jamaica Queens Public School 86...

I can remember running home from school on a Friday...I knew it was Friday because my mother would not allow me to play chess on regular school days. I would run down the green grassy hill, jump the fence, and go underground from one subway exit to another just to beat the traffic of crossing a busy city street.

"Why...are you...running.... so fast Cor..ey?" Tye asked me while huffing behind me.

"I am running so that I can be the first to choose my piece....white has a 0.9% chance of winning....all other things being equal you know!" I responded labouredly.

He knew it; and he knew it better than I did. He was a better chess player than me at this stage. I never understood the reason. I had great chess players in my family. He, being slightly overweight was slower than me. He would try anything to get me to slow down. He never got to pick his piece first. I had to use every advantage I had. He seemed to get the better of me most of the time though.

I played most of the weekend. I would play even when I went to see my grand-mother in the nursing home. It was more like a psychiatric facility. It would be the same routine every weekend. I would approach the desk...allow them to check my bag...they would locate the chess pieces...and ask me if I play chess. Just one weekend I wanted to entertain myself and say, "No I don't play chess, I am searching for Bobby Fischer, and I thought I'd bait him with these pieces in my book bag."

I really would have said it if I thought they would get the joke. The security would have probably looked at me like many others looked at me when I attempted a joke. Like a student majoring in foreign languages looked sitting in a third year calculus classroom.

When I finally arrived at the floor, just as I stepped off the elevator. I saw my grandma arguing with another resident.

"You talk so much you gonna run these people away from here and we won't have any one here to help us. You always actin' like a fool," my grandma said to one woman.

The lady responded as if she didn't even hear what my grandma had said to her, "How much is it...the real price? How much is it...the real price?" This patient's perseveration had gotten the best of my grandma at this point.

"It is enough to keep you talking! You got a brain, but it's packed away some-place and you never use it," My grandma yelled. At this point, I had to intervene, because the nursing staff was just getting a little to comfortable listening to this conflict.

"Hi grandma," I said, interrupting the argument.

"Hi Baby, how are you? Look a here ya'll this is my grandson the chess prodigy!" All the elderly persons in her circle say hello, even the lady that was arguing with my grandma...well, I mean...that my grandma was arguing with, said hello.

I sat down with grandma and played a few games of chess. She would always let me win a game or two. We both knew she could beat me, however her moves would be labyrinth, but discreet, in the quest of eradication of her own pieces. At times, it would catch my attention, and I would say, "GRANDMA!" She would respond, "Ohh baby grandma's getting too old for this game."

She *would* however, let me know that she was not too old when I got a little too cocky. Even after punishing me for my arrogance, she was proud because she saw a lot of her in me.

My grandma was the first unofficial female chess grandmaster in the streets. She played the underground for money. They called her, *The Queen Bee.* When I went into the parks, and told people I am the Queen Bee's grandson, they would all sit around and teach me new and amazing tricks. They would ask me questions like, "How's your grandma?" I would always be cordial and say she was fine. Of course, it was the truth, but that is not what they wanted to hear. They wanted to know about the myth.

A myth had spread throughout the underground. No one was certain on the validity of the legend, but like any good folklore, it was richly recounted. The legend proclaimed that the best players were summoned to play with the host. The legend also proclaimed that the host would send a mind walker to test a grandmaster's skill, by entering a board and moving the pieces. The best of the best chess grandmasters would eventually beat the board, and the mind walker would take them to the place where the games were played.

My father and our cousin Jimmy were also grandmasters. Jimmy was called "Torch" on the chessboard, because when he played the clock on any table, he moved so fast, it seemed like his pieces were on fire. We played table games all the time in our family. Any type of get together warranted table games. Holiday's like Thanksgiving, Christmas, The Fourth of July, and family reunions there were at least three tables going. A card table was assembled. This was where most of the gambling was done. They would switch from pokeno, to poker, to blackjack, to tunk, and then to spades. Aunt Barney would always make the money from the card table, and split it with my mom. They were always partners. At the dominoes table, my dad's friends would usually dominate that table. The players were usually islanders or old gangsters from the west coast. They played different styles. Sometimes they played by fives...

"If this ain't 25 I kiss you all ova, an if I miss yo' ass I'll start all over!" My uncle would say as he slammed the domino down, destroying the order, or how the pieces had been laid.

At other times, they would play to go out...

"Copicu, the rent is due, now put this muthasucka where ever you want to!" My dad would say, as he placed his last domino into the next player's hand. I never really understood copicu's or chuchaso's, but I liked to hear them play. Lastly, they assembled a chess table. The winner had a choice to play checkers or chess. There would never be anyone playing checkers unless a child wanted to play. It was not because they did not like the game. It was because no one could beat my grandma, not even Torch, and she never wanted to play checkers.

My dad would say when he lost to grandma, "I'm gonna get up so torch can put a light to your booty." And they would all laugh because they knew that there was no one at the party who could really give my grandma competition.

My grandma would say in return, "No you gettin' up cause the Queen Bee stung that ass, and you can't sit on it...now bring Torch over here, I'm gonna do the same thang to him. Maata Fact...Ima send'em back to the Statue of Liberty where he belongs, serving a big woman, like this big woman is bouta' serve him." The house would be roaring with laughter. Sometimes the police were called, but it would not bring an end to the clamor. My family knew most of the cops in the neighborhood, and some of them would actually be at the parties, in and out of uniform.

Somehow, my aunts and uncles would sneak one of the grands in to coax grandma into playing checkers. That would make her a mortal once again. Anyone had a fair chance to win playing grandma in checkers, and it would take her at least an hour to get the chessboard back.

The special chessboard had been set up in my room. It was a gift given to me from an old man for winning a tournament. We did not know each other at all. He said he had never seen anyone my age play the way I do. I told him that my family had great history and investment in the game of chess. The board was always ready to entertain players. No one played on it however, except me. It was my study board. It had nice marble pieces that were purchased in Tijuana, Mexico. There must have been something about the marble from Tijuana, because every time I wanted to play, I would have to remove a living beetle from the chessboard. It was very strange. I would spray the board and even wipe it down with boric acid, which did not stop the insect. I would threaten the bug with a shoe, but somehow he knew I would not take his life in this manner. The insect would not even budge. The window in my room had been open, so I grabbed the bug, threw it out of the window. To ascertain that the bug would not return, I shut the window quickly.

I would begin a game with myself, moving a piece and later returning to find the defense to the piece I moved. It was unbelievable. Who moved the piece? I started over, just to make sure that a piece really moved and it was not delusions of the mind. Again, I moved my piece and left. When I returned, the opponent's piece had moved. Then I thought to myself, it's my dad. My dad was playing with me! I was so excited; I quickly moved another piece, the white knight; however this time slipped and took a tumble to the floor. The piece should have broken into fragments, but it did not. It just had one chip in it, I believe from the fall. It just landed erect, as it had been placed there. At the time, I thought nothing of it. I picked up the piece, returned to the board with my move, and went outside. When I returned another opponents piece was developed countering my move in a sweet opening that was never played against me. I asked around the house if anyone had been moving my pieces, and received the same response from all.

"Are you mad? Your pieces are moving?"

That is when I stopped asking, word was getting around that I was strange and I did not want that reputation, I saw what it did to my grandma.

September thirtieth had come, and it couldn't have come one day later. I was ready for my birthday. My dad made sure that our birthdays were extra special. He took my mom and me out for the day. We saw a movie, went out to dinner and a play. The play was for mom, because she was not fond of the movies I picked out.

When we had returned home late that night, our home had been robbed. The place was in shambles. The pictures that were on the now missing wall unit were scattered across the floor. I was devastated. It was not because the burglar took everything, but because he hurt my mom and he broke my dad down. This was the first time I ever saw my dad cry. That day a burglar robbed us of our special moment. What started out to be the best day of my life turned out to be the worst. My mom howled. Oh, the way my mom howled…it was unnerving. She sobbed for what seemed to be all night long. The police came by and filed the report of everything that was taken. The big screen television and the wall unit that held the sound system. They even took the marble chess board that I had won at the tournament. Although my dad replaced the chessboard with an even more expensive set, I did not play on it a lot. It held memories of the loss that resurfaced every time I played on the board. Before I let go, I must add this day to the many that I saw my parents smile together. Unfortunately, it was their last. They separated six months later.

Chapter VI

On Tye's birthday, June 12, his mom gave him a party. He invited me, and a few of our other friends. I was still upset about my parents breaking up, so it was difficult for me to enjoy the festivities. It was a house party. His parents decorated the walls with shiny balloons of all different sizes and streams of colored paper were taped along the ceiling. A big multicolored sign read, "Happy Birthday Tyrone." The ice cream cake on the dining room table had the same message. The music was thunderous, playing LL's *Control Myself*, '*You got what it takes for me to leave my man.*' The children encircled the dance floor, which during regular domestic hours was the living room space, and began to dance. The boys took over the dance floor with their outrageous routines. The battle began as they started old school *popping*. It intensified as they go into *The Matrix*. Then it became unmanageable, as they began to sweat. The girls left the circle and danced near the dining area where it was a bit safer. The girls were proving that they too could do the *booty pop*, and *the tic*. When they started the erotic Jamaican style of dance, the parents stepped in and shut that down.

"It's time to cut the cake," Tye's mom said. She turned off the music, and turned down the lights. His uncle, Henry had the camera in one hand, and a cigarette in the other. With his belly protruding out from under the undersized white t-shirt, he was snapping pictures like a sleazy photographer. Because it was so dark, the reflection from his baldhead caused by the glimmer of candlelight was the only way we knew where to position ourselves for the picture.

We sang happy birthday to Tye. He made a wish and blew out the candles.

Tye began opening up all of the presents. He did not even wait to read the cards, until his mother stepped in and organized his opening process. She would take the card and read it aloud. If it had money in it, she would place the money in an envelope she had kept on her bosom. It was now time for Tye to open the gift his mom bought. Packaged neatly in leftover red and green Christmas wrapping, it was huge. Tye tore it open. His eyes opened wide. She bought him the expensive chessboard he had always wanted from the flea market. It was almost like the one I used to have. He hurried to put it away in his room. That small gesture expressed the quality of friendship we had. Although Tye loved the board and wanted to play on it, he didn't want my day to be any worse than it had already been. Only best friends would think of each other in that way. Even on *his special day*, he thought of me.

I forgot about the moving piece of the old chessboard until I graduated high school.

In our senior year, Tye and I earned scholarships to college and played on the collegiate level. We could not agree on the schools we wanted to attend, so we decided to register to rival colleges. I accepted an appointment at the University of Maryland Baltimore County to study medicine, and Tye accepted an appointment at the University of Las Vegas, to study engineering. We both were rated as international grandmasters in the first semester.

Tye and I continued to stay in touch, and would oftentimes play chess over the phone. We liked the phone…it was better than the internet, because you were not chained to the computer. Tye had even got better; and would destroy me every time we played. It was not his way to give a man a break.

We had a collegiate chess tournament, and hosted UNLV. When their team assembled in the library for orientation, I called Tye over and asked him if he remembered Nicky.

"Nicky played against us in grade school. I think you played for the thinkers…right?"

"Actually it was the Strategists," Nicky responded.

"I think I remember him," Tye said, although he did not.

"Can you believe we were once rivals and now we are teammates at the same college?" I asked rhetorically. Nicky was also a strong player, although his skill level was no match for either one of us. He was ranked an international master.

In the championship, UNLV beat us. Tye won the most valuable player award. This was the highest award in the tournament. I received the award for the most artistic combinations. Nicky was very impressed. He was much more impressed with my trophy than the championship trophy that Tye received. I never understood why, and did not think too much of it. Nicky did not win any awards in this particular tournament. Nicky invited us to his dorm room. I was instantly drawn to his board.

"Tye, look! Remember I had a board just like this one! Wow, I have never seen any one with another like this since we were robbed about ten years ago!"

"Now, Core…don't go crying like a sissy, you can't have that one, it has an owner," Tye said jokingly.

"No…you can have it. I want you to have it. My dad gave it to me…and he was murdered," Nicky said.

"Whoa, how did he die?" Tye asked inquisitively.

"He was shot by the cops."

"Damn, sorry to hear that," Tye said.

"Yeah man, sorry about that," I added remorsefully.

"It's cool," Nicky responded, like he was used to telling the story. After sitting and reflecting for a little while, Nicky said to me, "Corey, really dude, you can have it."

"Well, why do you want me to have it, didn't your dad give it to you?"

"Corey, you're the best chess player on our team, and I want the best to be with the best," Nicky chattered. I just stood there as if there was more to the story, and there was as he continued, "The board is just not for me. It makes me feel strange. I dunno, I can't explain it…the board just isn't for me."

Not picking up the clues, I accepted the board. When I accepted the board, I noticed the pieces. Oddly, his white knight had a chip in the same place mine had been chipped years ago. It was very weird. I said nothing more about the board.

I took the board to my dorm room, set it up, and sat on the defending side of the board. I sat there for an hour and just stared at the board. I waited for the board to make a move, but nothing happened. I felt silly…silly that I had fallen victim to my delusional behavior.

I got up and took a shower. As I was drying off, I looked at the board one more time. That damned beetle was crawling up the chessboard. As I went to get the shoe, pretending to splatter the bug, I noticed that the chipped white knight was developed in the beginnings of Reti's opening. I went to the door, and it was locked from the inside with the bolt and the chain lock. I looked all around the room, under the bed, and even out of the window. Being on the fifth floor, I did not think that a person would jump out of the window just to complete a practical joke. I sat at the board again and moved the b7 pawn to defend in the reverse Larsen's opening. It now appeared that the board was thinking, and not ignoring me, this was evidenced by the illumination of the board. It was clear that the board did not want to lose, evidenced by the time it took to move, so I went to bed and would wake up from time to time to make my move. In the morning, I knew that this was my old board. I could feel it.

Before the semester was over, Nicky committed suicide. No one ever understood it. He even left a note that shed no light on the subject to anyone...anyone but me. It read, "I was tormented by the moving piece."

We went to the funeral, and his mother was dressed in black. Her affect was appropriately flat, even though she had a good support team. His brothers and sister were in attendance. We paid our respects. His uncle came by and said, "I see you went to school with little Nicky."

"Yes, he was a cool dude," I responded.

"Well, believe me he will be missed," his uncle continued.

"Yes. He will. We played on the same chess team," I said.

"He was the best around his old neighborhood. His father bought him a board from NYC while he was away on a trip, when he was about ten years old. He loved that board. All he used to do was play. I don't think he ever lost on that board," his uncle remembered as he became teary eyed.

Not knowing what to say, I began to lie, "He was one of our best players."

"Yeah, I think he was gonna get rated as a grandmaster this semester," Tye continued the lie so I would not be alone. I looked at Tye nervously because Tye barely even remembered Nicky. Tye didn't go to our college. He just beat Nicky in chess when he came into town.

Tye and I had been rated international grandmasters in our first semester.

I enjoyed coming home at the end of the school semesters. The first thing I would do is show my grandma how I had improved. She was so proud of me.

"Grandma, they made me the captain of the chess team!"

"Oh babey, I knew you could do it. Do you talk trash too?"

"In practice I do, but we are not allowed in tournaments."

After a few games, I was the winner of most, the Queen Bee and I began to chat. I didn't think much of winning those few games we played, because my grandma always allowed me to win a game or two as long as I respected her.

"If you would play the underground you can say what you want, do what you want, and win as much as you want," The Queen Bee said as she stared at me sharply. I returned the eye, but her glare had an ominous twinkle.

I knew at that point I knew was truly a grandmaster. *My grandmother* would never tell me to enter the underground. She would always warn me about the hustlers down there. *For the first time in my life, I had not been playing my grand-mother. I had been playing the Queen Bee.*

We reminisced on the one time I did not appreciate my grandma's wisdom. We remembered it to this day, but this was the first time we ever talked about it.

"Grandma, do you remember the time…" is how I began…

A few years back in my juvenile arrogance, as I would say, in my juvenility, I thought that I was a much better chess player than I had been at that time. My grandma made it very clear to the family that I was not ready to play the circuit for money. It was just not clear to me. Some young guys in the circuit gassed me up into believing that I was better than the old men playing in Roy Wilkins's Park. It was the classic set up. They were underplaying while I was watching. Then came the hustle. When I sat down with my money, they would beat me and make me think they won with a lucky move. I continued playing until I was penniless. I was not only broke, but embarrassed. I had to go home and tell my grandma that I did not listen and lost all of my money to an old dude they called Darth Mal.

That, to me, did not sound like a good idea. I had thought of a better idea. I would return home, sneak into my dad's bedroom while he was away working, and steal money out of his jar in the wardrobe.

I noticed him placing money in that jar before and putting it in the closet once when he was drunk; but I was not supposed to know it was there. Of course, I never told him that I knew where the stash was.

I enacted the plan just how I had imagined. I snuck into the wardrobe, opened the jar, and pocketed about four hundred dollars. I went back to the park, and quickly lost that money too.

My grandmother, having hands like a construction worker, slapped my face hard when I finally came clean. She also scolded me severely. I was happy to be scolded by my grandma, because my dad would have killed me.

My grandma called up Uncle Torch and told him what happened. They did not have much time to execute the play. My dad was coming home this weekend. Uncle Torch and the Queen Bee began planning a way to get my dad's money back immediately.

They were rehearsing lines and practicing chess moves the entire night. They rehearsed until the sun peeked out of the night sky. My uncle went home and got a good day's sleep. Early that evening my grandmother stepped out to execute what was practiced. Before she left, I was forewarned that I was not to be in the park at all that evening. I did have friends though, and told them to report the play by play to me when they got a chance to call me.

Chapter VII

At the Park....

Uncle Torch had started early. He got some young college students in Bryant Park. He had won most of the money during the day, just a couple of hours before *their show* was about to start...

Torch had just stumbled into the marked park; the Queen Bee had been warming up the table for about an hour. Torch walked directly into the park and began to look for *the mark*. The mark was what the hustlers called the next victim. The Queen Bee gave him the sign so he would know whom to bait. Although, the park was crowded, no one was able to pick up on it.

Torch began to lean into the game being played by my grandma and Darth Mal; there was an obvious stench of liquor on my uncle's breath. He started into the hustle quickly as if he had to be home at a certain time.

"Hey, who let a woman in a man's game?" Torch said.

"What's it to ya?" Queen Bee says a matter of factly.

"Whas it to ya...wahs it to yah. Womenz don't play chess," Torch antagonized with a slur.

"We play for money over here," The Queen Bee said in tune. It was quiet for a while; a few moves had been played. It was clear to Torch that the Queen was downplaying her game immensely.

"I hope you got some, and not just planning to take mine," Torch responded later than the average late retort.

"Some what, Babey?"

"Money."

"Aww, Babey you still on that?" she continued to speak in a down-home Mardi Gras straight from Nor'Leans accent. She was on her last thirty seconds of the three-minute games. She snuck in a discovery on the King that Darth missed entirely. When he responded, his game was over. The Queen had about fifteen seconds left on her clock.

"Yo drunk ass was jibbering at the mouf so damned much that I lost concentration," Darth Mal Cried.

All the chess players at the table heard his poor excuse, and responded collectively, although not in unison, "Aww, man git yo' ass up, we don't want to hear that shit!"

"What did the barber say when he finished fuckin' up yo hair!" The Queen bellowed.

The crowd responded, this time in unison, "Next!" And they all started laughing.

As Darth attempted to make an escape from the table, the Queen Bee said, "uh, Darth, did you bump yo' damned head?"

Darth replied, "I got next," as he slipped the Queen a C-Note.

"They call me Sparks, cause I puts a light to yo ass!" Torch slurred as he sat down to play.

"Babey, give my man's your bid money," she responded ignoring his trash talking.

"Why, you don't trust me?" Torch inquired.

"Do you trust me? I am giving him the money just like you have to. Don't worry everything is on the up and up." She smiles as she pulls out her mini purse.

Torch takes twenty-five hundred dollars out of his pocket and gives it to the bookie, and asks The Queen if she can work with that.

"Aww babey, I ain't come out her' wit dat much, I got two thousand, but I will get the rest of it up." Before she could ask, one of the old gangsters dug the money out of his pocket to come up with the five bills she needed to contend. He knew his money was just as safe as it would have been if it were in a FDIC secured bank account.

"Thanks baby, I'll get this back to ya."

"No prob. Queen, do what you do."

The Queen Bee and Torch sat down to play. They played out the counterfeit moves perfectly. The moves, the costume, as well as the attitude made the hustle run fluently. The Queen took his money, while Darth Mal watched on with greedy eyes.

"Listen babey, take some sage advice from someone who knows. You *are* good, but you been drinking….and like that you are not gonna beat anyone in this park. Drinking and chess don't mix."

"I was just warming up. I know you not gonna walk with out giving me a chance to win my money back. Honey, I'm not in tha bidnez of giving back money, but I can give you some more advice…you paid for it, so that is the best I can do. If you want to play again, you have to put up some more money, and I think I took all that you had in your pocket."

"No, give me another game, my credits good!" Torch yells angrily.

"Not in this park." The Queen dropped the old gangster's five hundred and fifty on the table, then left.

Grandma came home and put the money back in the jar in the bedroom, before dad even knew it was missing.

Then, Uncle Torch really went to work.

"What's crackin' playa?" Darth Mal says confidently.

"Whas crackin', whas crackin'?" Torch mimicked, mocking Darth.

"Fifty dollar games, playa. If you do not have it…see tha man for credit or get off the table," Darth says strongly as he pulls his money out, staring the drunkard down hard looking for any sign of hustle, but not finding any scent of the game in him.

Uncle Torch pulls out twenty-five dollars and says, "Look playa, this is all I have. Put this with that an' let's play." They played. They played until it was obvious, to everyone except for Darth that the drunkard was no longer drunk. It may have been pride, or it could have been stupidity that kept him on a three-minute table that showed him no love at all for at least an hour. Whatever the reason, it was cruel and unusual punishment.

Uncle Torch cleaned up on Darth Mal. He allowed everyone else to win a low money game or two except Darth. Every time Darth sat down, he lost. He played until he could no longer get any credit from the old gangsters.

When Uncle Torch left, he had about six thousand dollars in his possession.

Every time my uncle Torch saw me, he laughed and laughed. I didn't know how to take it. Eventually after the first couple of days, I kinda got used to it. For those next two weeks, every time my uncle Torch saw me he would burst out laughing. He would laugh until the tears came out of his eyes. Sometimes my dad would wonder what was wrong with Torch, but every time my dad would ask, grandma would interject by saying to Torch, stop ackin' like a damned fool, and that would end it.

My Uncle Torch had a newfound respect in the chess world to me. I did not know he was such a hustler. My Uncle drank all the time, but was never really drunk when he went to the park. Everyone knew, or thought they knew that my Uncle was an alcoholic. He went to every meeting, made sure the streets knew the face, and he made sure that when they saw the face they associated it with an alcoholic. They never saw my uncle play because he worked another circuit. The family would never work the same circuit. It was just an unspoken rule. Another unspoken rule was to never let a hustler, hustle you out of your money. If you win it in the circuit that is good money, however if you won it by trickery, it was not respected.

It seemed like I would have learned my lesson, but I didn't.

"Grandma, you really think I have it in me?"

"Baaabey, you got it in ya!" She chimed back in that New Orleans accent. She then took off her cap, and put it on my head. I hugged and kissed my grandma, and ran straight to the park. I saw the same old cats that hustled me. I did not need Uncle Torch this time. I located Darth Mal. He knew who I was, and was smiling.

"Did you come to play?" He chuckled.

"I did," I responded as I returned a smile.

"You wanna get it on?" He said in a more serious tone.

"Absolutely." At this point, I sat at the table and turned the Queen's hat to the back.

I wasted no time. The three minutes on the clock was not enough time for him, but too much for me. I tore his ass out the frame. I beat him to the white meat; then left him painfully broke and looking stupid.

I packed my clothes, returned to the college, and returned to the college life. I took out my books and began to study. The study moment did not last long. There was a foreboding aura in the room. *The board*…it was calling me. I felt it in my stomach. I felt it in my mind.

I brushed the beetle off the board and began to play. I remember thinking to myself…does this beetle have anything to do with the moving piece? I dismissed the thought as soon as I pondered it. I made the next move with my piece. Usually, the game would be played over a series of days, due to the mental exhaustion of the middle game. This day it was not the case. We played the entire game. One piece after the other. The moves played by both sides were brilliant. Each time he made a sweet move, I would counter with another magnificent move. The best moves of my career of playing the board had been made on this night. The chess piece was moved and there was one less piece on the board. I thought to myself am I going to win this time? I never wanted to be this engaged in any game. I have never learned so much alone, or so I thought. I won. I was becoming great. Losing to the board in the past, I gained much insight. Chess players that defeated me in previous encounters became entertainment. Ten minute entertainment at their best, and now I defeated *the board*. I did not understand why the pieces moved all by themselves. But they did move by themselves, and if I knew it, then I knew it alone.

In my last semester, I had excelled. The world chess federation had rated me the number one player in the world. It had proven to be true as I won the World Championship, beating a dude they called Karpov. When I returned to the college, Tye's mom had called me. She told me Tye had some type of diabetic emergency, and that I should get to the University Medical Center in Las Vegas at once. When I entered the room, I had to get past the crazy lady in the adjacent bed. She acted as if she knew me. She kept talking to me and grabbing my hand. As I tried to be cordial, and gently slip my hand away from her, she screamed at the top of her lungs, "Your friend is in hell, but you have the power to get him out!" I freaked and yanked my hand away from her. The nurses came in and sedated her. They apologized to me for her behavior.

When I finally laid eyes upon Tye, he was in a coma. The doctor told us that he had fallen out in his room at the chessboard. They never found the person with whom he was playing. I thought that was odd. The person didn't call the cops or anything? What kind of friend was that? That person was no friend to him. Tye chose his friends wisely, and treated them well. There had to be more to it.

I sat there staring at an empty corpse, trying to ignore the crazy lady in the adjacent bed, as her medication was sluggish to take effect. I knew that the friend that I had was no longer in that body. My friend was somewhere, but it wasn't in this hospital. I didn't stay long. I couldn't. I returned to Baltimore and sat in my room. I had to get my mind off that experience. I looked at the board. The board returned the stare. The lights began to flicker, at that moment, the atmosphere changed. It was bizarre. Where I was once alone, I now had uninvited company. I…was not…alone. The aura moved the opening piece. I swallowed the anxiety that had rushed up in my throat. It came right back up. My heart racing was the only sound I could pick up, even though my ears were giving my heart unmatched competition, working harder than they ever did. The apparition had moved my pieces many times before, but this time I was terrified. I was alone. For me, things had changed. The apparition had a tone of horror. I didn't want to play.

It seemed as if the board could sense my fear. The board continued to place my heart at a state of shock. First by moving its pieces. Then by throwing the pieces at me for not responding to the moves. I tried to run out of the dorm, but the door would not open. I screamed like I was getting a wax job...to no avail.

The ghost escorted me to an unfamiliar place.

Chapter VIII

The Ultimate Challenge...

You ask why the board has summoned you. I shall respond to your inquiry. I am Subvidious, also called the host. I am the keeper of the board. You are the first world champion to be invited to the sector. The previous person who was in possession of the board was not invited to the board. The board drove him mad. He eventually killed himself. At that point, I understood exactly of whom he was speaking. It was about what happened to Nicky.

Subvidious produces a contract out of thin air. It gravitates as he reads it. An ancient looking fountain pen topped with the feather of the buzzard was hovering along the side of the contract.

The contract read...

You have been selected to participate in the ultimate challenge.

This agreement is entered into by and between two parties The Demon Child, referred to in this agreement as Subvidious residing in the Sun, and Corey

1.   Anthony Kent referred to in this agreement as the Pieceslayer addressed at PO Box 1908; New York, NY 10163

2.   This is a game of chess. The rules are as follows:

a.   You have a total of exactly 24 hours to play one game. 12 hours on each side. The clock begins on the first move.

b.   If you run out of time, you lose. It matters not if you are winning by points.

c.   There will be no draws of any type, only wins and losses.

d.   You can use the pawns to get any piece you want as many times as you want it, except for another king.

e.   If you summon the beast, you must be punished.

f.   Once the first piece moves, the contract is binding.

The beast was like a safe haven. If you summoned the beast, he would appear and destroy the game that was being played, and since the games were not recorded, it was like a wild card. No one knew who summoned the beast at first glance. The card was pulled if a loss was inevitable, but it did not come without consequence….

When the beast came out, he murdered the person who summoned him. The beast would take the player to their limit on the pain threshold, although they would not take them over that point. It would cause them to expire. The game had to be finished. One had never summoned the beast more than once. When death was felt, it was never forgotten. He carried a flesh-eating whip, and swung it like the hammer of Thor.

As I continued to read the contract, I saw the fine print.

The fine print read…

The first life force to lose two games has lost the challenge. The loser will forfeit the soul that resides within them.

This was the consequence of losing the best of three games? I thought to myself…only three games? Is that it?

"The best of the best in the greatest mental game in the world have never declined the ultimate challenge. The benefits outweigh the risk. If there is such a thing as risk for a player of your caliber," Subvidious said enticingly. He continued, "The previous world champions were rather weak. They could never stand up and defend, or challenge for that matter. The real champions play in the underground; they would not be allowed to play in the tornaments of the world. You see just like everything, even chess has its politics. You would think that they would want the best to play the best. However, if you are the best but have no money or no sponsor you will never get your chance to shine, that is just how it is in your world. It is not the case here. In this arena, if you are considered the best, you have earned a chance in the ring. It matters not how much you own or where you are from, as you can see, many of the opponents are not from your planet. No one cares about how large the other person's brain is or what this person's rating is at the time he or she sits at the table. It's not important here. We do however make the game fair. If there are changelings, or mind walkers, or any other type of individual that could have an unfair advantage over another we dismiss those specialties when they enter the sector," Subvidious states charismatically.

"How is that done?" I asked inquisitively.

"I am not privileged to show these things...however my master is trustworthy and you have his word that all will be done to assure a fair game," responded Subvidious.

"I am from New York City, home of the dishonest. What good is your master's word to me subhidious?"

"It's Subvidious. And the word is in the contract," he said with a strange smile that could have been mistaken as a sneer.

"Well, I don't think so subhideous," I said again, remembering what my Grandma told me about the hustle game.

"I think you'll change your mind when you see this. Subvideous opens the gates and shows a sphere. The sphere shows Tye imprisoned. His mind is shackled to the board. He wants to be set free, but he cannot leave. He continues to play chess in the dungeon at the top of his game.

"How in the hell did he get in there? They said he had a coma, because he was a diabetic. He was in the hospital, I saw him!" I said as my voice got louder.

"Yes physically. He never told you about the chess game that he was given by his girlfriend. She got it from an old man."

"You set us up!" I screamed wildly.

"No, I just gave him an opportunity! And Tye had the balls to take it. He just didn't have the skill to get what he came here for, but you.... You can change that. You can use the skill given to you by your gifted family. It's innate in you...save your friend!"

At this point, Tye was horrified. I never saw Tye in such a state of disarray.

"Corey, please don't do this...decline the offer!" Tye begs. Tye then tells Subvidious that he wanted to play someone else.

"What do you want to do?" Subvidious says to me, ignoring Tye's challenge. I contemplate. Staring at Subvidious, staring at Tye. Then looking at the glimmering board....I make the opening move.... E-4.

The board screams in unison with Tye in the hospital bed, "NOOOOOO!"

Chapter IX

Career Month…

"Hello, this is Ms. Adaire. May I speak with the parents of Nicky please?"

"You're speaking with Sergeant Major Nick Keaton, ma'am. How can I help you?"

"Well this is career month for the students, and I sent out a letter asking all of the parents to make an effort to participate. I never did receive a response from your household."

"I am terribly sorry about the break in communication Ma'am. I did not get the memo."

"Are you still in the Army?" Ms. Adaire inquired.

"I was never in the army ma'am. I am a former marine. I have been retired for about twenty years now."

"Wow. That's amazing! Well on behalf of the faculty, we would like to thank you for your service to this country. Do you think you could speak to our children about your occupation? I am sure it would be very interesting."

What time do I report for duty?"

"Well I have many spaces available…"

"I'll be there today at fourteen hundred hours," Sergeant Keaton says curtly as he slams down the phone. Sergeant Keaton goes into his closet and pulls out his white class A uniform, that had been professionally cleaned and heavily starched, and his military shoes, which he immediately started to spit shine. As he looked at himself in the full-length mirror on the inside door of his walk-in closet, he noticed something was missing. It was his saber. The last time he wore his uniform in public, the police found it necessary to confiscate the weapon. In order to rectify the regulation discrepancy, Sergeant Major Keaton just removed the holster and commenced with the duties of the day.

As Sergeant Keaton was preparing himself for career day, Ms. Adaire was also preparing. She had invited a famous musician to speak on Career day, although she had prepared for the event, she had no idea what was about to happen.

"Okay students we have a special treat today. This special guest has sung background for the late, great, Luther Vandross. He has also played keyboards for Maxwell and Will Downing. This person has also played the backup keyboards for great bands like Maroon 5 and Train. He is now a renowned solo jazz musician. Let's welcome the proud parent of Erika and Derika Love…Mr. Xavier Love." Mr. Love walked to the front of the classroom with one hand in his pocket, the other holding the keyboard. He had this cool kind of swagger. It looked like a more polished version of the strut Nicky was trying to perfect. He got to the front of the class and took his time setting up his two pieces of equipment. A wireless microphone and a keyboard.

"Thank you. It's like…a pleasure to be here man…I mean like a real pleasure. School is like, where I learned to play the keyboards. Don't be a fool, stay in school. Make Love…not war, because…Love is a battlefield. Yeah, its like…loves a battlefield." It was obvious he was skeed up…coked out…snow-blown. None of the students in the classroom knew it, not even his daughters. They just thought he was cool. Ms. Adaire noticed something wasn't correct, but she attributed it to a lack of schooling. She was still happy to see him. She actually became a big fan after Jennifer surprised her with an autographed copy of his CD.

"Ms. A, I'm taking requests. What do you want me to play, I'll play anything…except chess-my babies drive me crazy with that shit," whispering the latter part in her ear as he laughed to himself.

"How about something from Prince?"

"Cool. Which songs? Give me three."

"Okay, how about, *Purple Rain, Slow Love, and Sometimes it Snows in April?*"

"Cool. Let's rock!"

The keyboard came alive as soon as he placed his fingers on the keys. It was a jam session. After the warm up, he started taking requests from us. We began shouting out all of their favorites. *Yeah* by Raymond Usher. *All for you* by Janet Jackson. When he played that, his daughters jumped up and said daddy, please play *Unbreakable* by Alicia Keys and *Shake it off* by Mariah! Of course, he granted both of his daughter's wishes. Then he went to Michael, and played *Beat it.* We were all dancing like Usher, Michael and his sister Janet in the classroom. Even

Ms. Adaire was dancing with us. Ms. Adaire was doing the old school dances. We were surprised. We didn't think Ms. Adaire knew how to shake it off. We were laughing so hard, we started to cry. He played for at least thirty minutes. X-Love could play anything. He ended the jam session with Ms. Adaire's selections. *Purple Rain* was the grand finale.

Mr. Love had sweat beads on his forehead as he packed up his keyboard. Ms. Adaire thanked him again for his time. He put his hands to his lips, made the peace sign with his fingers, and then blew a kiss letting the peace sign float from his mouth. When he was done, his hands were stretched out like Christ on the cross, still displaying the peace sign. That is how he stayed, as the classroom went wild. They shouted his name X-Love, X-Love. Then he picked up his equipment and left. It was so cool.

As Sergeant Major Keaton made his way out of the house and into the street, his neighbors looked in awe. He politely smiled and bowed courteously, as he assumed that they were staring because his uniform was without blemish. Although it was, this happened to be the last thing on the mind of his neighbors. They recalled the last time he was dressed in his military outfit...

It was during the Veteran's Day Parade. Sergeant Major Keaton was asked to participate in uniform, representing the retired veterans. As they marched, an anti-war protestor shouted derogatory comments from the sidelines. In the beginning, the man was ignored. They ignored the protestor until he screamed baby killer and threw a beer can hitting Sergeant Keaton on the side of his face. Once that happened, Sergeant Keaton lost all military bearing. He broke formation and pummeled the sideline commentator. The man attempted to return the blows, but was unscuccessful. Before he knew it, he was curled up on the floor gasping for breath. Sergeant Keaton placed the man in a deadly chokehold, and locked it tightly upon his neck veins. As NYPD approached Sergeant Keaton, other veterans broke formation. These veterans attempted to obstruct the officers from assisting the protestor. They had formed a barricade around the street fight.

"Sarge, you gotta let him go," one officer said as he fought his way through the military blockade. In a matter of minutes, blue coats completely filled the city block. The police were everywhere.

"Move out of the way, or you will all be arrested," another officer shouted.

"This is your last warning people! YOU WILL BE MACED!" the officer in charge had blurted out in an attempt to disband the blockade.

The police eventually broke down the military barricade. It took a few cans of mace, as the veterans would not go down easy. Many bystanders were injured. It quickly escalated into a massive casualty incident.

"This man called me a baby killer…Ima make him a liar!" Sergeant Keaton screamed.

"Sarge, let him go! Now! LET HIM GO NOW OR YOU WILL BE TAZED!"

The next thing heard was the screaming of that same officer, as Sergeant Keaton sliced the officer's thigh with the saber. At that instant, Sergeant Keaton was tazed by another officer. The tazer not only shocked Sergeant keaton, it also shocked the officer with the injured leg, as he was connected by the saber's blow.

NYPD finally regained control of the parade, and involuntarily admitted Sergeant Keaton, and many of his military brothers to Bellevue hospital for evaluation. Although he was released after two months of treatment, his saber was never returned to him.

Mr. Keaton continued making his way down the street until he arrived at the schoolhouse. As he walked in, the principal met him at the door. His uniform afforded him full public school honors. As he signed the guest book and showed his identification, the principal escorted him to Ms. Adaire's classroom, and Ms. Adaire was made aware of his presence.

We were all excited after X Love's performance and could not wait for the next parent. "Students we have one more special guest here today. He has fought in many conflicts to include the Vietnam War, and many other conflicts. He has been awarded various medals for his service to this country: The Purple Heart, The Bronze Star, and The Expert Marksman Ribbon. I am pleased to introduce to you, Nicky's father Sergeant Major Nick Keaton." As Ms. Adaire introduced the sergeant, Nicky's eyes opened wide. It was clear that he wanted to say something, maybe give a warning, but his mouth would not formulate the words. The children clapped and awaited his entrance. No one entered. Ms. Adaire announced him a second time. Still, he did not make an entrance. Ms. Adaire walked over to the door, to see if he had been detained. Sergeant Major Keaton mimicked a loud explosion with his mouth. Then he jumped into the classroom and yelled get down! I said get down! Charlie's a comin' and he don't kill wit no bullets, he jus like ta sneak up on ya wit tha bayonet and gutcha! Now hit the damn flo'! There was not one person standing, not even Ms. Adaire. Ms. Adaire hit the floor so fast, her glasses flew off her face.

The children noticed Mr. Keaton at once. They did not know him as Sergeant Major Keaton. They knew him as the crazy man. His entrance confirmed their knowledge of him.

"In war, real soldiers are born to fight, trained to kill, ready to die, and never will. ARE YOU LISTENING?!"

A few of the kids to include little Nicky responded, "Yes."

I CAN'T HEAR YOU! I SAID...ARE YOU LISTENING?!" At this time, the entire class screamed in unison, "Yeessssssss!"

"Good. War is a terrible thing. A soldier lurks in the shadows, and kills anything that moves. I am gonna give you something to think about. How would you like it if they took off your arms and legs and kept them as souvenirs? Huh, how would you like it if someone picked you from out of a platoon and hung you in the streets? Huh? How would you like it if someone spat in your face? That wasn't Charlie. That was America! America did that to their soldiers. When we returned, we wasn't concerned about Charlie...We was concerned about Americans. People like you and me!" The school security heard all of the clamor and rushed into the classroom. They were about to have it out with the sergeant until Nicky stepped in. "Grandpa please. Don't hurt anybody. These people had nothing to do with it." Nicky then turned to the Ms. Adaire and said, "My grandpa is sick. He's shell-shocked. I gave my mom the paper, but she just threw it in the garbage," Nicky said to defend his granddad. The paper he was talking about was the notice of Career day. Mrs. Keaton never read it.

After the police and the paramedics subdued Sergeant Major Keaton and took him away, he kept saying that he was an American Fighting man. He would not reveal any classified information, and he recited some type of serial number. He said that repeatedly as the emergency personnel escorted him to Bellevue hospital for another evaluation. That memory will be branded in my mind for a long time.

Afterward, Ms. Adaire tried to calm the class down. When she finally got the class to settle down, she asked the security to stay in the class with the children until she made a phone call.

She called Nicky's home and told Nicky's parents exactly what happened.

"Kay, this is Claire, Nicky's chess coach. I also happen to be the dean for his classroom."

"What happened Claire? Did Nicky get in trouble?" Kay asked in a worried tone.

"No Kay, not at all...He actually was a big help today. The fifth graders were having career month. Every morning, in the auditorium, we have parents speak about what they do on their jobs. I called your home thinking that I was speaking to Nicholas's father, but it wasn't. It was Sergeant Keaton. He said that he would come down, and I had no idea..."

"I know, I know…he seems to have all his good sense at first glance, but he has a screw loose honey. My husband thinks that if he takes his pills, that he would be fine, but if that were the case, he wouldn't have a regular bed at the VA psychiatric Hospital."

"I understand, but this incident could have been avoided if you would have taken the time to read the letters that I sent you. You're son needs your participation. It makes it difficult to provide a good education when I have no support from the parents. Can you tell me why you don't respond to any of my letters that I send home?" An uncomfortable silence overcame the phone conversation. "Hello?" Ms. Adaire said, as she did not get an answer the first time.

"What letter? I don't believe I received any letter?" Kay responded.

"Nicholas told me he brought the letter directly to you and you threw it in the trash…now if you don't agree with my suggestions Kay, I am willing to listen to some of yours. We just need to communicate."

"I don't have a problem with you or any of your suggestions, they are fine, I am just too damned busy." Kay hung up the phone.

"Hello? Hello?" Ms. Adaire was furious that Kay would hang up the phone in her face. Ms. Adaire redialed the number, the answering machine picked up. Ms. Adaire hung up without leaving a message. She sat at her desk, pondering what went wrong in the conversation. Ms. Adaire finally understood the challenge. She went to her classroom and attained her recorder.

The bell rang and it was time to go home. No one moved however until Ms. Adaire returned to dismiss them. She returned with the reminder letters to give to the classes.

"Remember to remind your parents that we are still doing Career day and we would like to see the parents that promised to come, so if your parents said they would come, let them know tomorrow is the day. I will have breakfast and other refreshments for the parents as they set up to present. Nicky, sit tight I have something for you," Ms. Adaire said. This is a CD I made for your mother. Please give it to her."

Nicky went home and gave his mom the CD. Mrs. Keaton played it.

"Hi Kay. I have taken the liberty to put all of the special events on this CD in chronological order, so that it would be easier for you to attend some of the school functions. 1. There will be a chess practice every Monday, Wednesday, and Friday after school at approximately 3:30 that will last for one hour…" Ms. Adaire had recorded her voice listing Nicky's entire school schedule to include the extracurricular activities and practices.

Kay called Ms. Adaire after school and left a heartfelt message on her answering machine.

"Ms. Adaire, this is Kay-Kay…this is gonna be pretty hard for me, that is why I waited until you went home. I want to apologize for my behavior. I got the disk you sent with Nicky. Thank you so much, you are…"

At this point Ms. Adaire picks up the phone, "Don't mention it I'll see you at the next chess competition."

"You sure will Ms. Adaire," Kay said surprised that Claire was still at work.

"Nothings changed, we're friends Kay, please call me Claire," Ms. Adaire said warmly.

You sure will, Claire. Talk with you soon."

"Take Care." And they hung up, this time in agreement.

I went home only to be harassed by my brother.

"I saw LaShawn today, she was looking gooood. She asked about you," Shawn said.

"Really?"

"Nope. I'm lyin'," Shawn chuckled, stomping his feet on the floor as if what he said was the funniest thing happening.

"Dude, how dumb is that?" I responded as I went upstairs.

I did my homework, and played a couple of games of chess with my brother, both of which I lost.

Mom was first to return from work. Dad came in soon after. Mom prepared dinner for everyone. She then took her time to clean up after everyone. The condo was spotless.

Roman went upstairs took a shower completed his ritual and went to sleep. His mind began to drift off into dreamland…

Chapter X

Walking with the Sun, the Yakoda Healer said it was prophecy. The United States government said that it should have been monitored more closely. The world Health Organization said it should have never been created. The beast gave birth to the weapon, and the weapon gave birth to destruction.

The War of the Reservations was on its 29th month. The battle had been bloody. The adversaries were exhausted, and welcomed the end of the war. The Yakoda warriors were fighting with everything remaining, and were effectively defending their reservation against the Protectors of the Planets Strategic Air Force (POPSAF).

The ancestors favored the Yakoda Warriors with their success in battle. Their stamina overturned the balance of the revolution. The Yakoda Warriors were just at the end of the bloody journey, and their tactics were advantageous. The POPSAF were wearing down. They did not have the endurance of the reservationists.

The cultural dances and rituals of the reservation did not end as the war continued...The women danced alone...not by choice.... they would never dance without their male counterparts; but their men were protecting the lands during the season of the dance. Although, the young girls did dance with the boys that were too young to join the battle. Two young girls stood out in particular. Young in age, but women by marriage. They were Cheyenne and Eve. Cheyenne, the chief's daughter, was a thirty-six special. This unsafe, but rather sexy pistol had been missing a caliber or two all of her life. Eve was her wild sidekick. They were best friends and well known for their dance. At the age of seven, they began dancing in the fairs. Now both being married and at the ripe age of sixteen, they were unable to grow out of their silly antics, making spectacles of themselves for the sake of the creative freedom of dance. These girls were rebels and looking for a way to express themselves that would not being taken as so offensive that they were kicked off the reservation.

"Eve, you ready?"

"Would you just go Cheyenne, and hurry up before your dad changes his mind."

"Turn on the radio," Cheyenne said. At this time, both girls are smiling the teeth right off their faces. The music began; it was old school rap music. *Dancing Inferno*, by fifty-cent. The girls rip off their dresses, revealing the forbidden spandex. They dance. They dance in synchrony. Unprecedented hip-hop moves, explode from their hips.

"Look at my dad Eve; he can't get enough of it. We're killing him!" Cheyenne huffed as she let the spandex fly. She was right. She was killing him, but it wasn't a good look. The chief had his head down, and appeared to be ashamed, for the fiftieth time. The only difference was that he was getting older and his tolerance getting short.

The Chief got up, stomped over to the music box, and brought about its sudden death. Cheyenne and Eve just looked at each other in confusion. They were clueless.

"Dad, dude, what did you just do?"

"If you do not get out of my face, young lady I will kill what I love the most!" Cheyenne continued to look at Eve for understanding. Eve offered none.

"Get your rubberbonccuses out of here!" the chief resounded with a raised fighting tool, also known as his walking cane. This was the same tool he used to bring silence to the music.

The girls picked up their dresses and rapidly exited the dance floor. These were the not the first, nor the worst sneers and gawking eyes they received, they were used to the looks. What they were not used to was their dad, getting so upset. (Eve thought of the Chief as her dad also, he took her as his own daughter when her father was killed. He even gave her away when she got married.) He was not a short-tempered man by any means. How could he be with those two for daughters? He let out a sigh, returned to his chair, and continued the ceremony.

The indigenous Corybants completed many versions of the rabbit dance. In the performance of this dance, the males danced like peacocks. They wore the plume of the bird on their outfits. The Peshaw quills, or the quills of a porcupine, were also worn. The young males jerked as they pranced around in circles radiantly. The females were much more reserved. They danced from one side to the next bouncing on the balls of their heels.

The boys led the Sundance. The sun dance was a dance used in conjunction with the war dance. In the war dance, the more feathers you saw, the higher in position you were. The type of feather also gave you a higher cast among the Yakoda. An eagle feather was the highest feather you could place on your headdress. Once the Yakoda males had a certain amount of feathers, or at least one of them was an Eagle feather, that warrior became a celebrity in the tribe. An Eagle feather on your headdress was like a medal of honor.

The Yakoda Indian was a very humble, yet fierce warrior. The Yakoda warrior would peel the skin off the expired adversary and prepare the flesh for the ancestors. After the flesh was prepared in a particular ritual and blessed by their healer, Walking with the Sun, the flesh of the enemy was then placed upon a tree in sacrifice for the ancestors. In return, the ancestors were to find favor in their struggle.

Combat through the mountains made it too easy for the Yakoda at this point of the war. The weaponry ignited flames that illuminated the sky. As the night fell, the horizon continued to bear light.

"Take this to hell wonkdey!" Walk through Fire said to the soldier from the space team as he ran through him with the soldier's own glowing saber.

Smart arrows, arrows that could be set to direct locations by heat sensors and explode upon impact, pierced directly through the eyes of Yakoda Indians.

The POPSAF's arsenal was sophisticated, but at this point, had little effect on the outcome of the war. They were losing the battle. The POPSAF wanted a new weapon to change the tide. Dr. Cody-Lynne Calle, the note-worthy Nobel Prize winning physicist, unwillingly, was responsible for most of the weaponry the POPSAF possessed. A scientific-technical genius, and a female with the power of *seeing* certain aspects of the future, developed the newest edition to the healthcare world. She already saw herself winning the Nobel Prize for the Orb before it was awarded to her. The orb was a highly sophisticated spherical object, that most resembled a soccer ball due to the divisions of the orb, or *the eyes,* as Dr. Calle would call them, attempting to bring a human touch to this technical structure. This piece of equipment would change the course of medicine. It would definitely change the outcome of the war. It was proven to alter the atoms, electrons, and protons in a cell. This newfound technology was very important to the science world. This breakthrough could change the cellular structure on its own as long as it was properly programmed. This meant the cure for cancer, the cure for aids, and the cure for ultimately any disease that is manifested by the alteration of the basic units of life.

When the military got wind of the orb, all they could think about was a weapon of mass destruction. "The Cody-Lynn Orb" had the power to do just that sort of thing. The government, without understanding of the orb, invited Dr. Calle to a conference…

"I would like to present to some, and introduce to others, our special guest invited by the President. A scientist who has consistently supported the military with her advanced weaponry. Without further ado…. Dr. Cody-Lynne Calle," a presidential aid declared, as the table politely applauded her presence.

"Thank you. I am pleased to be a guest at your conference," Dr. Lynn said as she stood up and quickly returned to her seat.

"Let's make this thing short and sweet. Dr. Calle, you will begin mass production of this orb so that every Special Forces soldier can add it to their equipment," the president said hurriedly, seeming as if he had other important issues to contend with at the time.

"That would be impossible Mr. President. I, nor would anyone else be able to mass-produce the orb, unless the first one was destroyed. A delicate phenomenon exists regarding the chemical and physical properties of the orb…it contains a meta-nucleic radiation…"

"Why would that be a problem?" He inquires rudely as he interrupts her complete thought.

Dr. Cody-Lynne, being a technical speaker attempted to change her style of speech to eliminate confusion. "Mr. President, developing two orbs in a finite radius would destroy the balance of the universe. An atypical energy displacement would ensue. Not only would that deactivate the individual weapon, but it would also mutate the collective abilities of the weapons to cause a devastating meta-nucleic radioactive endothermic reaction. This theory is somewhat similar to the black hole phenomenon. It would force energy into this planet at a phenomenal rate, thereby causing a rearrangement of the solar system and the end of life as we know it…in other words, the Earth would convert from being a piece in this vast universe, to becoming the center of the universe…"

She continues as if no one is getting her message. "The Earth would have the energy of the Sun!" She says excitedly to no response. "This complex reaction is respected by scientists because of its highly destructive capabilities." She says in exasperation.

"Uh, I see," the president retorted, but he did not. Neither did any of the members that were present at the special conference…see.

"Well Dr. Calle, we are prepared to make you an offer for the orb. We'll appropriate its use for military operations."

"Mr. President, ladies and gentleman, I am an adored scientist. Although, my creations have been utilized as such, I do not make weapons with the intention of mass destruction. I would ask that when you or your members invite me to a conference, that I be allowed to educate and provide lecture. I would even assist the military in finding treatments if not cures for the new biological weapons. I just do not want to be a part of genocide. True scientists are lovers of life. And with that, I offer you all a good evening." She gets her things and exits gracefully.

Chapter XI

The POPSAF knew that they were losing the war. They also knew they were going to make use of the weapon. Knowing that Dr. Calle would never agree to the use of the orb for war purposes, they contacted the Strategical and Tactical Assault Theater or as it were more commonly known as... *The STAT team.*

The STAT team was responsible for dramatic rescue of the World's greatest chess player during the world Olympics, Corey Kent, *The Piece Slayer.* That incident was the first time the public even knew that the STAT team existed. What the public did not know was that the STAT team was responsible for masterminding an excessive amount of unethical assaults at the command of the government. The latest request of the POPSAF would be no different. They contacted Col. Gaitlin. Col. Gaitlin got on the horn to General Williams, the STAT team commander. General Williams already knew his request before he could inquire.

"This is Col. Gaitlin reporting, requesting special permission to engage in secure line transmission directly to General Williams."

"Col. Gaitlin, this is SSgt. Collinsworth. I am the gatekeeper of the STAT team. In order to grant you access, I need you to respond to my pass code."

"Go!" Ordered the Colonel, sounding like a Drill Instructor.

"One....two...niner....niner," reported SSgt Collinsworth.

"Blackjack," the colonel responded.

"Niner....niner...two...one," retorted SSgt. Collinsworth.

"Comedian," the colonel responded.

"Access granted Colonel. Stand By."

"This is General Williams Go!"

"General, Good Day Sir…"

"Cut the bull Gait. I know what you want and it'll cost ya! I will get the weapon if you send me about four or five of your men to take the fall. You know that I can get my men into anywhere, but the world will be looking for the ones who pulled this caper, and my men cannot be exposed…ever. I need a few good men to take the rap. If you can provide the man power, we're in bid'ness," the general said convincingly.

"I understand…I have never failed you and will not now. I will have them report to the disclosed location in 72 hours, at exactly 2300 ZULU."

"We will be expecting them. Make sure you tell them that they won't be returning home," General Williams said gruffly.

"Will do Sir," Colonel Gaitlin said remorsefully.

Back at the war of the reservations...

The POPSAF called for reinforcement. The friendly forces assembled to assist in the battle were former allies of the Yakoda warriors. The promise of money can make a nation of people do strange things. With the Protectors of the Planets Air Force's newfound allies, the Cherokee Indians, the Yakoda Warriors were no longer a match for their adversaries. The technology of the Jody-Lynn orb proved to be excessive. The tide of the battle changed.... The POPSAF demolished the Yakoda warriors.

The War of the Reservations was over. There had been no mercy on the survivors. The Protectors of the Planets Strategic Air Force (POPS-AF) had ransacked the village. The POPSAF and Cherokees ran through the Bad hills claiming all resources that were not grounded, even the women. They took great pleasure in pillaging the land. It was like a badge of honor to their fallen comrades.

The POPSAF slaughtered all the Yakoda that attempted to surrender, which were not many, until there were no Yakoda men standing. The massacred Yakoda warriors were survived by their women (many of them pregnant), and their children. The widowed females had to pick up what they could manage and abandon their homes. The widowed Indians had to trek in one great pack, knowing that the POPSAF would go to very drastic measures to destroy their culture, or at the very least, their way of life; and they were right.

Many of the Yakoda women knew that they would be violated, and they were ready. Taking the blade used to sheer corn from the husks, the Yakoda women hid the weapon under their long skirts. That very evening when the Cherokee Indians came to attack, they were met with resistance. The Cherokees burst through the first open door. It was rigged. A homemade explosive detonated as they entered the home propelling glass, and pieces of metal into the torso of the enemy. Although not all died from the blast, many were disfigured for life. Metal shrapnel penetrated the lungs of many without flack vests, causing sucking chest wounds. Others caught fragments of glass with the glove of their orbital space.

The enemy that overcame the blast, and continued the advance into the homes of the Yakoda encountered a bloody massacre. Some of the Yakoda women slit the necks of their children from ear to ear while the young were asleep. After the mercy kill, they prayed for forgiveness to the ancestors, and then they committed suicide.

The pregnant few that got away, returned to their soil a few days later to see their villages destroyed. They shrieked when they saw the blood of their loved ones. The blood spilled across the land painted the story of their untimely demise as a poet's pen to paper. Slaughtered bodies were everywhere.

When Cheyenne and Eve returned, they searched for hours through the spoils of war. Eve was first to find her husband. He had been captured; it was apparently before he could take his own life. He was a sniper. And as a reminder to all who fought against the side of the POPSAF, he was hanged on the very tree he took refuge to eliminate the enemy. Eve was shattered; Cheyenne felt her pain. They cried and at that moment Cheyenne said, you will no longer be known as Eve, but as **Fortitude Scorching Eternal Arrow.** The name represents the way your husband's arrow traveled to terminate the enemy. Not very far from that sight did they find Cheyenne's husband. He was gracefully executing the dead man's float in the river. His eagle feather still intact upon his headdress. He still had the enemy's head in his possession as he floated over the waves. Eve consoled her best and only friend at that moment. Cheyenne was devastated; of course, Eve knew of her pain. They cried again, Eve said as she got her courage, you will no longer be known as Cheyenne, but as **Murdurqua Kills in Water**, as it represented her husband's energy in the liquid element of life.

The shocking display of how the warrior's bodies were not respected changed the docile women forever. The women became savage beasts. They regretted not entering the battle and dying along side their husbands. They each took on a new name representing their husband's warrior history, his actions in battle, and death.

From the slaughter emerged the greatest female nemesis the enemy had ever known. They called themselves **Sunka Witchakassa** pronounced shoonka witch-a-kasa. This word translated into bitch fighters to all that encountered them. They made a vow that they would never be violated, captured or defeated while they still have breath to fight. It gave new meaning to *Death before Dishonor.*

The Yakoda Warriors had been favored again by the ancestors. The very thing that changed the tide of the war was now in their possession. It was the Cody-Lynn Orb. The orb had been recovered by Fortitude, the widow of Scorching Eternal Arrow, one of the mighty Yakoda snipers. The orb was found in the bosom of a deceased POPSAF Airman. He must have committed suicide or made a grave mistake, her guess was the latter. She was not going to make the same one. Gingerly, she grabbed it, being careful not to cause disturbance to any eyes of the orb. She placed it in her sack, and fled before anyone could see her.

Due to the misuse of the orb, the land was no longer viable; and without the assistance of the orb, the land would not host vegetation for another twenty years.

The Sunka Witchakassa warriors or Bitchfighters were made to explore new territories. They chose to leave the planet Earth, and find others who would have mercy and accept their children.

They settled upon Zandor, which was adjacent to Xalanus. Zandor was known to be the birthplace of the changelings. Changelings were individuals who in their original form appear as one-eyed beasts; however, they can change and usually will alter their innate form to mimic the form of the creature in their presence. They did this at will and could camouflage themselves for an exponential length of time. It was as easy for them to blend (that is what they called it when they changed) as it was for a human to clench a fist, just as long as they can keep focus.

The Yakoda clan set out to find the Baron of the changelings. It did not take long. They were actually led to the palace by a young changeling. He had been hiking along the same unfamiliar, less traveled road.

When they arrived at the destination, the clan was surprised to find that the palace was not a palace at all, but a cave. The cave however, was tremendous. The journey through the cave was like a maze. And if a person did not know exactly where to travel, then they would find themselves depleted of energy and starved to death, as the corpses scattered throughout the cave had proved.

As the clan entered the sanctuary, they were stopped by the guardians, and taken to the Baron.

"Who is the leader of this clan? Step up and be recognized," inquired the Baron of Zandor as he sat on a throne laced with shimmering jewels.

"It is I my Lord, Murdurqua-Kills in Water, named after my late husband, a true brave Yakoda Warrior in which the ancestors gave him favor in any natural environment of water," the great warrior Murdurqua responded in a very humble manner. She was positioned with her head bowed, knees bent, and arms stretched before her, her palms facing the floor, as was her head.

"What part of the universe do you hail from?" Demanded the Baron.

"My Lord, we are from the planet Earth, land of the United States."

"You may rise and explain the reason you have solicited the help of my people."

"My Lord, we are victims of a massacre. The POPS-AF infiltrated our clan, and hired an army of our allies to bear arms with them and destroy our land. Being that we are widows my Lord, we had to give up all of our possessions; that is the way we mourn for our dead husbands. The beasts took advantage of that, and ransacked our reservation. After they finished pillaging there was nothing. They took our property, our belongings, our pride, even took what could never belong to them, I am ashamed to say my lord, she said with her head bent down in embarrassment. These people are evil my Lord and must be destroyed. The entire planet is in jeopardy. The healer prophesized that this was the beginning of the revelation. If we do not take action now, it could be the end of our universe! This is a very important plight and we must pay attention to the signs."

The spiritual healers were greatly respected throughout the universe for their healing powers and their ability to engage the future in the present time.

"Bring forth the healer man who told you of this prophecy," said the Baron of Zandor.

"It is I, Walking with the Sun, my Lord," he spoke aloud as he entered making space through the crowd with his staff.

"Speak your prophecy," the baron said with longsuffering curiosity.

The prophet began to meditate. The entire atmosphere of the safe haven changed. The electrical equipment flickered, as the power was being drawn unto the prophet. The lamps at the throne went out completely. The locks worn by Walk with the Sun rose from his shoulders, up above his head. The pupil of his eyes had disappeared. In a commanding voice, the prophet spoke.

"The beast will arise, giving birth to the weapon. The weapon has sight, but not through the eyes of man. The weapon can see what most men cannot. The weapon must be stopped. It will have a chance to be destroyed in battle. If the beast is not destroyed then the prophecy of the end of humanity as we know it will be carried out. One female in our clan will have the weapon, but will fail to destroy it."

When the people heard the medicine man recite the prophecy, all clergymen fell to their knees. The clan and changelings followed the actions of the clergymen.

The same prophecy had been inscribed in their secret books. They knew that the truth was being deciphered.

The clan of Bitchfighters and their children were welcomed with open arms. This was very rare, because anywhere else that a losing clan attempted to start anew they would not only have to give away all of their possessions, but they would also have to kill all of the male children. This was not negotiable to the Bitchfighters, and it was never asked of them by the changelings.

"Is this the weapon that you seek?" Fortitude shouted out from the crowd. She pulled the weapon from her sack and held it up in the air. Everyone fell to their knees.

"Bring the weapon forth," commanded the baron. After holding and admiring it for a moment, he threw it to the ground to try to break it. Not one scratch came to the orb. He then put the glowing saber to it. At once, it consumed the energy of the saber, and gave heat to the entire cave. Inside the cave, it was 130 degrees Fahrenheit, and getting hotter. The entire room was scorching. There was an alert called; and the fissure, evacuated. They thought the orb would explode. It finally cooled down approximately two days later. The Baron held a meeting with his militia...

"General, I have called this meeting because we need a soldier to complete a mission," the baron said secretly.

"What is the mission, my Lord?" The general responded.

"I would like to speak to the soldier alone. No one is to know of the mission, not even you general. It will only bring complication to the mission. I trust that you have someone loyal that we can count on to complete the mission."

"I will send him to you at once Sir," the general stated respectfully.

A young changeling named Rhaffaar entered into the baron's quarters. The baron was expecting him. "I am Rhaffaar my Lord," General Lore asked me to proceed to your chambers.

Without hesitation, the baron got straight to the point. "I am commanding you to keep the orb."

"What Orb, my Lord?"

"This one." The Baron pulls the orb from his robe, and shows it to him. "This Orb is the weapon that will destroy the world if we do not find a way to stop it. Your mission is to hide this orb until you can find a way to destroy it. You must find this Dr. Cody-Lynne Calle, the scientist who made it, so that she can destroy it," the baron says to Rhaffaar, looking deep into his eyes for any sign of hesitation.

"I accept the honor, my Lord." Rhaffaar returns without delay. Knowing the art of war, Rhaffaar knew that this was one mission that he could not refuse. The acceptance of the mission meant danger and possible death. The refusal of the mission meant certain death.

"It comes with great responsibility. Many soldiers of the universe will be chasing you. It requires you to leave your family and be in hiding and in constant motion," the baron whispered aloud as he looks around his quarters for any sign of espionage.

"I understand my Lord." Rhaffaar accepts the orb from the baron and places it in his knapsack.

"Also, do not disturb the orb unless death is the only alternate choice."

"Yes my Lord," Rhaffaar stated. And with that, he was dismissed.

The Bitchfighters took a newfound adoption for the same abhorrence POPS-AF that the changelings had for many years. These females practiced war operations as their husbands used to practice. They became fierce fighters and hunters, to the death. Through the generations, they regained their male warriors in their tribe, but they would no longer stop the females from fighting. This was the process of evolution in their culture.

The Bitchfighters trained with the men. Their name was infamous. Murdurqua held received many honors for her warfare throughout their reign as a newly emerged warrior tribe. They had earned the reputation of one of the fiercest warriors of the galaxy…male or female. Some would say you had a better chance dying respectfully if you engaged the men in battle. The females saw too much; they had too much hate in their blood. They would never forget how their male counterparts died…fathers, husbands, and brothers at the hands of the enemy.

These new breed of fighters, for years to come, would go to many parts of the world regaining land. Overtaking it from their adversaries, just as it was stolen from them.

"The time is now!" Exclaimed Murdurqua. "We must take back what belongs to us. We have Fortitude a Special Forces spy, trained in the art of assassination. The female warrior who has infiltrated the POPSAF. She has done her job well. She will receive a king's ransom and a veteran's parade when she returns. Who other than the sexy Fortitude could have infiltrated their craft as a laborer? She is our greatest weapon."

The crowd cries out, "Forty! Forty! Forty!" The mood is intoxicating. The energy in the room alone could light the night sky.

"You all will have your chance at revenge! Soon we will avenge our fathers, our lovers, our brothers, our uncles, even our cousins and grandfathers! They will rue the day they ever crossed us! We are the Yakoda Warriors! We are the Bitchfighters!"

The crowd is out of control. They spar with each other. They grab their weapons and put on a show for Murdurqua. She is proud of their skill and knows that they are ready to go to war a second time with the POPSAF. This time the outcome would be different.

They grab their weapons and move out to the land of the double crown.

Chapter XII

Ten years after the first war...

It all ended almost just as it began in the land of the double crown. The day was coming closer to the end as evidenced by the brim of sunrays peeking through for one more glimpse at this side of the world. The day scorched, we were burnt, and the burns of the desert were unforgiving. The pyramids made the twilight appear regal. Unfortunately, the only warriors that appeared regal this day were the Bitchfighters.

This had been the longest most energy expending battle that my crew had to endure. We fought the entire day; and had been holding ground, but they were relentless.

The enemy was determined to find the doc. It was like they knew her every move. Dr. Calle had been under our protection since she expressed concerns on her life three months ago. During her weekly ritual of fasting and meditation, she was forewarned that her life was in danger due to the Orb being in the hands of the enemy. She thought we could protect her. She was right. Although this particular military unit's operation did not include civilian protection, I allowed the mission to be bisected. My motives however, were a bit different than what she had expected. She had a seer's knowledge, and I thought we could use her. I was wrong.

She had been ordered to stay closely beside me. It made her sick, and me at ease. She being a vegetarian, and I being a blood-loving carnivore, we really did not mix at the chow hall. We really had nothing in common, except the love of *her* life. I thought that it would work in my favor, understanding how opposites do attract. However…I was to her, as bug spray was to an insect that just would not die. She was subjected to my conduction at social hour, in the field, and even in my quarters (although there was only one bed in the bone room, she did not have a problem letting *me* sleep on the floor). I did not allow her to leave my sight. To me, it was more than a job. I was attracted. She was repulsed. Although she felt that way, her higher classed upbringing, affability, and unexpressed fear of my command, never allowed me to experience her distaste.

The enemy had advanced. They backed us up to the southern part of the Nile. These were no ordinary fighters. We discovered this at the most inopportune time. They were the crème de la crème of savage fighting, the Bitchfighters.

As the sun was dismissed, the black clouds entered the land, and so came the rain, fast and furious. The lightning was thunderous and unrelenting. It traveled sideways across the horizon, and over without ever touching ground. The tide had begun to turn for the worst. It was de ja vu. My men were exhausted having fought since the early morning and were being run down quickly.

Fallen airmen scattered around the land, like shaken up dominoes. The doc and I were not far behind. She followed my lead blindly, as the lenses of her spectacles were crushed in the retreat. My men could no longer protect us. We ran until we could no longer evade the enemy. I crawled around in circles, trying to face the enemy that formed an arced position before us. Behind us, the plateau was just a few feet away. I was depleted. Not having enough energy to resist, I welcomed any adversary that came. Death behind us, and a perilous precipice ahead of us, I came upon the vision that ended my quest. The vision that I may be able to describe to the corpses that lay beside me soon enough. The great female warrior, which I had seen before, but knew not, was tormenting my defeated body. She shot the weapon from my hand. She destroyed it. It was useless after her direct hit with the pistol. Ignoring the hysterics displayed by the doc, she grabbed my flaccid body, and pulled me by my flack vest up above her, approximately to her crown. Her talisman shining light in the last bit of sight I have remaining. I am gazing down on her like an oversized jacket. I could not see the warrior well, as my vision was blurry. Every now and then my eyes would grant me a focused look, at which I closed my eyes in disbelief. This was one strong bitch!

"You will beg me to stop the rain; you will beg me to end the pain. I am the great Bitchfighter…. Murdurqua, Kills in Water, the true warrior of this battle."

She stood at least 6'8 could be more; It was hard to tell from the angle that I was hinged. She had muscles like a man…. A strong man. She was cut especially in the arms. Her body was large; she was big, but not fat. She had energy for days.

Her stamina was unmatched, even by my warrior strength. I was no match for her fighting style.

"I am not scared, I love these men and I shall die with them!" I responded as I gazed upon the red of her eyes.

"Ok, then I shall call you wonkdey the crazy warrior. I will still have no mercy upon you." She continued to say with a pride all her own, "and the one that you trusted…the one who infiltrated your force was a Bitchfighter. The great female fighter who witnessed her slain husband in the fields with four smart arrows to the face…She named herself Fortitude and her clan was named Shot with four arrows."

Then approached this female menace. She showed her ugly face upon my range of sight…It was very painful. *I knew her* "You are the servant girl. You work for me. Do you not?" I inquired in disbelief. *This is how they knew our location the entire time.*

"I *am* the one you seek so badly, but I never worked for you, lechone," growled Fortitude.

"I thought you would have seen enough of me. I expect that you are ashamed of your heart, the heart that gave way to your destruction. It was not me, but your own heart who betrayed you. You know your history. How could you think that I could *ever* slave under a member of the POPS-AF? While you were so busy trying to fuck the nerd, I was sabotaging the mission the entire time…right under your very nose. She continued as she spat in my face…Your crew destroyed my entire world the only thing I ever loved, the only thing for which I would gladly die. I showed you mercy. The same mercy that your team proved to be lacking. I allowed you to live. Now your luck has come to an end."

It was crazy, but when Fortitude spat in my face, I could taste that bitch's blood in my own blood. I did not believe that death would be so bittersweet. This hatred allowed me to live a little longer. Yet another warrior repeatedly pierces me with a weapon I could not discern. I just would not be left to die with honor nor dignity. I could see the demon fowl above waiting to eat me into Hell. I could not give them the satisfaction at the present. Unable to keep the promise of protection to a scientist, of whom I have displayed an unspoken love, I was incensed to the point of madness. I whispered in the doc's ear.

"This is the end of the road Cody." She knew something was wrong, because he did not call her doc, or any other thing she considered appropriate for a commander to say. I called her by her first name. It frightened her, as well it should have. "I am ending your life so you can die with dignity," I said in bewilderment.

She was terribly confused. She tried desperately, although futilely, to escape her protector, the one who once proclaimed a love for her life...now wanted to take it. He placed her in a death choke, more specifically a neck scissor with his forearms. No one actually knew what was going on. The bitchfighters thought he was holding her hostage. They were not concerned at all. However, it did give him time as Fortitude expressed her apathy towards her interpretation of his hostage situation. He prayed.

Dear god of strength and endurance, I come to you in humble and embarrassing position. I have never feared death...in fact I welcome the challenge. Master I have tried to honor your will and do what is right in your eyes. If it is my time, I am ready to die. I just ask that the God that I serve does not take a great warrior like me at the hands of a Bitchfighter...I do not deserve to die like this. I deserve to die with honor. I have served and protected in the name of God. I have made mistakes in my life, as any man has done, but a punishment like this is too great to bear. I request my God, MY GOD that you just give me enough strength to end my own life...

God heard my prayer. Something very strange happened to me. It took over my body, and I felt like I was in autopilot.

Split second…

I…I did it.

In that one split second…

The black clouds had a silver lining. They had given me strength.

I got up the final bit of energy that I could muster, grabbed the doc as she screamed, scratched, and clawed me to her death, and I jumped…

The jump was more like a limp hobble over the cliff. It was all I could manage. I cheated Murdurqua! She wanted to kill me, but I beat her to it! Cody's episode of syncope made it easier to hold her close to my body as we tumbled gracefully into the next life. The horizon changed colors. It went from a bluish grey to dark blue to a dark gray again. The horizon was red because the sun was not to be forced out of the sky. Thunder in the clouds sprayed the earth like a spider's web. The rain poured down relentlessly. Each sheet of rain would catch up to me as I was falling and strike my face, the blow from the sheets of rain were welcomed. It was like balm to my wounds. It soothed my pain. I began to feel my consciousness leaving me. I began to speak to myself…

I was closer to death than I was to living. HAHAHAHAHAHA. I was confused, I did not know why I was soo happy to die, but still I was elated. In my maddened state, good judgment was a stranger to me. I had plenty of choices…I could have fought to the death, a rule that I live by. I could have been submissive; at least I could have pretended to be submissive until I found a way of escape. I could have, in my warped since of thought, bit her. I could have bit her in the face. I could have blinded her! Bit out her eyeball.

My body is numb, I feel no pain. The rush is nauseating…It sickens the mind, it sickens the body. I can see visions, out of control visions. Visions of life. Visions of death. Some visions I welcome. Some visions are uninvited. The visions of my mother and me playing in the snow…Helping my sister put on her ballet shoes for her first recital. I could see me teaching my brother how to ride his bike…and him falling yet another time before the concept sunk in and he was no longer afraid…I could see my grand father coming home from the War on Iraq, one of the rare times I saw him smile. My eyes envisioned the proudest moments in my life…The birth of my niece Caramel, and being decorated with the Medal of Honor as a commissioned officer in the POPSAF. My mind traveled to the most challenging times of my life, the altercation between the league and the Bitchfighters, the time when the war began. The time when we were deployed to their lair. Where I had lost my weapon at the most vulnerable, most unwanted time of the battle. My eyes saw the lowest times of my life, the first time that I had ever cried as a man. The time I was defeated by a Bitchfighter. The intense moment lead to my imminent demise. Then came the pain…I killed the woman I loved. I saw the painful death of my sister by her psychotic lover...the only thing was...My sister was still living. I saw into the future...I saw the fall of the towers a second time, and the death of thousands of innocent people. I saw me...enjoying the bittersweet blood of my enemies spilt. Then in that, one split second the vision of my death or at least attempt at it.

Chapter XIII

Chasing the changeling...

In an instant, the sky split and The Saxon comes screeching through the sky. The Saxon, named after Bethesda Saxon, the mother of the great warriors of the Roman Empire and Camelot times. Caramel Gatlin and Chance two young officers in the Protectors of the Planets Strategic Air Force (POPS-AF) materialized from their battle craft, The Saxon, onto a busy park, and they began scanning for the changeling. She is here somewhere, I can sense her, Chance said with confidence as he spoke of the changeling.

The park was huge. The day smelled brisk, the gentle winds blew from the northwest, causing leaves to rustle in a mild Tasmanian spin. Tall green ferns were outstanding as they populated the area. They were not alone as the squirrels and woodpeckers made a home in their bosom. There were many trees that gave the air a certain scent, the grass a certain color, and the foliage distinction. The blades of grass were well groomed, although the leaves that took flight from the trees made that same well-groomed grass look unkempt.

The children were in abundance. They were not aware of the splendor of the world, the masterpiece of God that gave the original form to this great park. The only stimuli the children accepted in their awareness were the animals. They tried earnestly, but rather futilely to give chase to the city creatures; the same animals that the swiftest four-legged predators would have a difficult time bringing to submission. The children were even unaware of their own parent's observation, unless their names were called that magic number of times. It was quite loud in the park, but it was loudness known all too well to parks of that quality. The sound that was heard became the chatter of the birds, singing to their own beat. It took the form of the dogs barking uncontrollably at the squirrels that they could no longer chase since the trees put a halt to their progress. It was the cats screaming, to get down from the trees that they ran up due to the mistaken belief that the dogs were chasing them. It resounded as the mothers' tone as they were screaming for their children saying don't play so rough, and the kids were responding, "okay mom" although their pledge was not sincere. It clamored as children screaming, as they were running, at the top of their lungs, at the top of their speed respectively. The children were just screaming, screaming for no reason, no spankings were handed out, no bad people chasing them, just good old fashioned screaming. I guess to add to the excitement.

Chance and Caramel took it all in. Chance knew what they were both thinking. This is not going to be easy. They both looked at each other as did a quarterback and a wide receiver looked when it was forth down, they were down by six, and there was just enough time for one more play. They looked at each other that one last time before the break in the huddle.

Chance, a mind walker, set out first. Caramel set out right behind him, but not in the same direction. As Chance honed in on the playground, Caramel searched the park where the animals were being fed.

Caramel circled the park frantically. She also knew that she had not much time left to find her uncle, Col. Gaitlin. Call it niece's intuition, or call it a military intuition, whatever the case she had this feeling. She scanned the area thoroughly, piercing into the eyes of every life form that could possibly be the life form that they spent most of their journey searching. She came across and old man sitting on the bench feeding the squirrels. He was a tall, lanky, and gracefully aged gentleman. He sat wearing a dark colored brim hat with a lighter shade feather. He appeared a bit disheveled by stress, but not dirty. Caramel sat down and with her sweet and unattacking smile began to talk....

"Sir, I am Capt Caramel Gatlin from the POPS-AF, and I need to ask a few questions if you don't mind. Are you from this area?"

"Yeah, I lived here all my life, but I can see that you are not from around these parts," he said with a chuckle, observing their uniforms and their demeanor.

"So you know most of the children and people that come to the park?" she followed, ignoring his comment.

"I think so," the old man responded. "I come here almost every day, and the neighborhood knows me. They call me Mr. Wiggs, I guess my entire name Wiggertanovich is too long for them, he said with a deep-rooted chuckle. The young children ask me to play sometimes, and their parents are very friendly to my wife and me."

"Where is your wife now?" she asked inquisitively. A moderate pause followed.

He said tearfully, "She is in the care facility now. We lived alone....and I just couldn't take care of her anymore. But I go to see her everyday," he said redeemingly.

"I am so sorry to hear of your wife's condition and I hope that things will be fine with her," Caramel said with no emotion. Offering no sympathy or a tissue for the waterworks, she continues to report.

"I want to explain to you why my friend and I are here. You see we are looking for a thing that does not belong. The thing is a changeling. I know this is difficult for you to understand, because it is rather difficult for me to explain. The being is able to change into many different forms of life...and the only way for a human being to realize that she or he is in their presence is to look in their eyes. The color of their iris will be blood red. Certain creatures can smell the changeling, and other special beings can sense a changeling. That is why chance is here. He can sense this thing. We are hunting him down to bring him to justice. We have pursued the beast through approximately eight different planets. Planet Zenith is the last place he was located. We fought, he resisted, was wounded, and again he fled. I need to know if there appeared to be anything strange that you observed while you were here...."

Their conversation is overcome by children in the park. You could here the children, none of them older than ten years old, playing tag, a running as if there lives were in danger. A few children began arguing over how an oldie but goodie song was to be sung.

"No, Heidi, listen! It goes like this! My neck, my back, touch my body just like that," one young girl said.

"NOOOOO, like this my neck, my back touch my privates just like that!" Another responds.

Not to be outdone Heidi jumps in the girl's face and says in the melody of the song, "You're wack, smoke crack and act stupid just like that!"

All the children begin to laugh at Heidi's silly chants.

Chance being a mind walker, could feel that he was on to something; however the signal was distorted. The signal would always fade when he was under stress or the subject was clearly aware that it was being tracked, and therefore would do things to be evasive. The park was a great place to be evasive. The scores of minds that Chance would have to penetrate discouraged him. He was also worried; not only because of the difficult search, but he also sensed that he had not much time left. The critical reason to locate changeling was not just to bring him to justice, but also to disable this Cody-Lynne Orb that prevented stable materialization. Doctor Calle addressed the basics of the orb with the team before she went into protective custody. Col. Gaitlin was still out there dying. Chance knew the colonel was dying, he could feel it. He also knew he could not expose what he felt because of Caramel's delicate heart.

Chance sensed the changeling, and honed in on the feeling…Caramel saw Chance focusing and communicated a standby request to the craft.

Meanwhile the changeling, who had transformed once again, began to make friends. The beast had changed into a child. This time it took the form of a cute little girl with curly hair and dimples to match. She had on a blue and white uniform, the kind that you wear during class at Catholic school. On her feet, she wore black and white schoolboy oxfords. She blended in perfectly, except for one thing. The gigantic slash upon her head that was dripping blood on to the tip of her black and white schoolboy oxfords. The bruise on her forehead appeared to have dazed her, as she stumbled around trying to fit in with her new environment. The beast covered her head with her scarf and kept her hands clutching her head to try to disguise the bruise. She quickly sought shelter with her newfound sisters that were jumping double-dutch. Awkwardly the beast attempted to jump double dutch. She attempted, however it was a poor attempt at the sport.

Heidi who observed the misfit jump in the double-dutch ropes began to lash the beast with her tongue.

"What's tha matta? Are your legs broke?" Heidi exclaimed in a jovial manner. She continued to say, "What are you, the Taliban or something? What is that rag on your head for?"

Heidi pulled the rag off the beast…and screamed in horror.

"AHHHHHHHHHHHHHHHH, what happened? Oh My God, what happened to you?"

"SHHHHHHHHH!" said the beast but it was too late. Both Chance and Caramel heard the screaming and were on their way, weapons drawn.

"There are some people following me, I think that they want to kill me," the changeling said to Heidi.

"Oh my God, your face is bleeding, why don't you go to the police?!" Heidi continued to shriek.

The changeling responded in a defeated tone…"They sliced my face with a laser. It is too late…the police can't help me now…no one can."

That instant Chance was upon the beast and flexed his weapon. Caramel tried to clear the playground. Since the beast could no longer pass through hyperspace, he meditated. The changeling had enough energy for one last transformation. He began to transform.

The beast changed into a monster that was unknown to this planet. It emerged from a little child of 4 feet 7 inches into a beast. The beast stood 10 feet tall, and towered over Chance. It did not last too long as the changeling was exhausted. Once Chance charged the laser to a lethal limit, the beast returned to his original cyclopsed form and came to a rest. The changeling went from a beast, to coward, without energy due to the disabling injury. The last encounter that the changeling had on the planet Zenith with the POPSAF, left him severely injured to the frontal lobe.

The beast gladly gave up the Cody-Lynne in exchange for its life. The Cody-Lynne was deactivated and the unit aboard The Saxon was made aware.

They materialized the colonel and Dr. Calle's flaccid body in mid air. The few airmen that still had remote signs of life were also picked up. They were received in the bay by an emergency medical team that transferred them directly to the medical theatre. Dr. Calle was dead. Somehow, the colonel, in his poor state of consciousness, knew that she had died.

The beast knew he did not complete his mission. The weapon had secrets…secrets that held the key to ending or prolonging life at a cellular level. He failed. Later that day the beast would not fail a second time. He finished the job the POPSAF began. The changeling took its own life.

Chapter XIV

The Catch...

The team working on Col. Gaitlin was assembled specifically for this purpose. An elite team that consisted of a medical doctor, a nurse, a medic, and a man at arms. The doctor was a 65-year-old female fireball from Texas named Paris. At the age of sixty-five, she had the body of a forty year old and looked no older. Paris was new to the team, and she had never really worked with a crew before. Being the most skilled on paper however made her the team leader. Dash, the nurse was a seasoned veteran that worked with everyone except Paris. Dash, having been a flight nurse before the Kitty Hawk accepted airtime, was the most experienced in theatre. He had seen a lot, more trauma than any one in the crew. His leadership and good judgment proved his skill level every time under pressure. If a life could be saved, there was no better chance than having Dash suited up in the theatre. The medic was a cerebral juggernaut named Erica; they nicknamed her Dearie, because she was so amiable. If there was a procedure to be done, she knew the technical jargon. Erica developed a profound vocabulary, and could report any complication to the higher echelons and decipher their responses quickly. Although she would bore you to death with the tautology, she knew most if not all the medical diagnoses and the systematic procedures that complimented the diagnosis. This saved a lot of precious time needed for life-saving endeavors.

Lastly, the man at arms, Shogun. They also called him Sho'nuff, because he would sho nuff show his weapon if any problems broke out on the craft, not to mention he fought like a ninja. At the age of forty, he was looking forward to his retirement. He was the sentinel at the door of the theatre, to assure nothing would stop the life saving mission.

"We need the Orb up here stat!" communicated Shogun.

"It's on its way, Sir," Chance responded.

In the theatre…

Once passed Shogun, you were in the theatre. The theatre consisted of the entire emergency labyrinth. From that main entrance, one could go from the initial emergency rooms, to the medical rooms, to the trauma rooms, and also to the operating rooms. Each of the rooms had team members. Although the team was highly capable, it did not always come with a human touch. Many rooms had pods. These were androids that were specifically named by the type of medical situation to which they specialized. They were specifically identified by the humans on the team that utilized their specialty. The team would assign a special name to the pod. Almost like a nickname. That particular pod was then specialized to a team, which was more specific than just being a pod specialized to a room. All pods were coded to take orders directly from any authorized medical team personnel.

Pods were always in the area awaiting directives. They were precise. They were diligent.

"She is received with a cessation of all life signs," Xanax, the surgi-pod determined.

"She's not dead until she's worked on and dead Xanax. Prepare her in operating room four with the surgi-pods," responded Dr. Paris. Xanax began working on her at once. He hovered above her and covered her face and chest. Dr. Calle was completely covered from the torso up by Xanax's transformation. He placed a tube in her, gave her oxygen, and began defibrillation. Immediately, life-saving CPR was being performed. She was transferred to operating room four, where Xanax and the surgi-pods completed the preparation as ordered by Dr. Paris.

Dash reported, "The colonel continues to lose pressure. I can't get a line in him. He is fighting like a beast…sedate him already!"

"We already injected him with 10cc's of ativan…that dose would put down the average lion," retorted Dr. Paris.

"We need to get in em' now, to stop the loss," Dash said.

"He is talking about an invasive sur…"

"I know what the in tha hell he's talkin' bout Dearie, I want to secure him on the breather just in case this ativan kicks in first, so uhm, do ya mind?" Paris responds.

"Dearie set the vent to deliver a tidal volume 15ml/Kg, High flow Oxygen, mode SIMV, with minimum resps 12, PEEP at 5 cm of water 2 mmHg negative inspiratory force," Dash rattled off.

"Yeah, what he said, and record peak inspiratory pressure, minute volume, carbon dioxide pressure, oxygen, and PH level." Dr. Paris adds.

As she wipes the perspiration from her brow just above her glasses with the forearm her left gloved hand, Dearie repeated the orders. After she received confirmation, she carried out the orders with minimal difficulty. Then she put out her hand and blurted out, "Change!" An emer-pod who is assisting, changed her contaminated glove.

Dr. Paris was extremely satisfied with the team she commanded. She felt as at ease as a doctor could possibly be in the theatre. It was like they had worked with each other for years. No one was offended by her cussing in the theatre; in fact, it made them feel more comfortable. They knew she was not tight, stuffy, or an ignorant doctor who slept her way to the top of the theatre.

Dr. Paris continued to allow Dash to lead. She felt comfortable with his capabilities. It also freed her time so she could work on Dr. Cody-Lynne Calle. Although Dr. Cody-Lynne was in another room, the surgi-pods had prepped Dr. Calle and had been awaiting instructions by way of telemetry. This new age technology made it easier to do more with less, which was one of the many mottos of the squadron. Dr. Paris typed the coordinates in the computer then placed her hands in specialized gloves that would mimic the actions of the surgi-pod she activated. She began the surgery on Dr. Calle. The surgery was intense. The combination of Dr. Paris's knowledge, Dr. Calle's will to live, and Xanax getting serious, not to mention a shit load of atropine, caused the flat-line to transform slowly into a bradycardic rhythm. Blood pressure 50/20. There was a great sigh heard throughout the theatre as everyone watched. This was a better sign, but she was not by any means in the clear. Still not breathing on her own, the bradycardia became agonal. The blood pressure again was almost non-existent. She was dying for a third time, a second time on the table. It was already two hours in, but Dr. Paris refused to give up. Exhausted, she ordered a blood typing, and transfused two pints of blood into Dr. Calle. In the fourth hour, the blood pressure went up second time to 66/40. The team, in their relief, began to cheer and clap. They knew that they would be able to stabilize Dr. Calle with that pressure.

The residents from the Air Force Academy were in another operating room working on the other airmen. General Lawz, a surgeon general who was famous for his controversial study on genetics in the operating room, served as the attending for this mission.

After two and a half intense hours of delicate surgery, Dr. Paris knew that the mission was almost complete. In theatre, as the crew is finalizing, she begins to joke.

"Your Doc is hungry, get her some lunch!" Paris barked out, testing the staff.

"Get it yourself," Dash responded without anger or animosity, passing the test.

"I can't get anything to eat. I'd have the entire naval corp. there. I'm a good looker!" she responded as everyone laughs.

"She's a keeper," Sho'nuff says aloud, with his arms crossed over his chest.

"I guess our work is done here. He's gonna make it," said Dr. Paris.

"Close him up," Dash says to Dearie. Dearie winks, and nods the positive as she had already begun to close the lac.

"Yeah and close up Dr. Calle too. The access key is on the computer," adds Dr. Paris.

"Is the computer gonna take my prints?" Dearie inquires trying to catch them before they leave.

"I put in the entire team's prints…even Sho'nuff's, so you won't have a problem," Dr. Paris said. Dash pulls her by the arm out of the theatre, so they can get something for the team to eat.

There were no casualties on the Saxon that day.

Well, they deactivated the orb and saved the colonel. What about the prophecy?

"The beast will arise, giving birth to the weapon. The weapon has sight, but not through the eyes of man. The weapon can see what most men cannot. The weapon must be stopped. It will have a chance to be destroyed in battle. If the beast is not destroyed then the prophecy of the end of humanity as we know it will be carried out. One female in our clan will have the weapon, but will fail to destroy it."

The weapon was not the weapon that the alliance thought it was; the message was decoded incorrectly. The weapon was not a thing, like the orb, although it was a weapon. It was not a man, like the colonel, although he was a weapon and has the power of foresight. The…the weapon was a woman, you see. Dr. Cody-Lynne Calle was a seer…she had to live…to bring the prophecy to life…and bring forth the revelation of destruction through her inventions.

Chapter XV

I jump up out of bed, and look at the clock. It is nine forty in the morning. I rush to put on my clothes, grab my books and rush down the steps. I am met by my brother eating cereal and watching the cartoons.

"What's today?" I inquire.

"It's Saturday boner…now put your books down you freakin' psycho," Shawn says as he laughs.

"Shawn, what happened to your eye?"

"I had a fight last night bro, the guy did not appreciate me putting my tongue in his girl's mouf. He's lucky that is all she got," Shawn said, as he was proud of his battle scar.

"Dude, why would you do something like that? Did you know her?"

"Nope. She was hanging behind the school where we were drinking, and she told me they were just friends. She even gave me her number. The problem was she told her boyfriend that her cousin was hanging out with us and she was going to go say hi."

"Well…was her cousin hanging out with you guys?" I asked.

"Nope. She told him it was me. I guess we were kissing cousins," Shawn snorted as he smiled.

"Why did he want to fight you?"

"Look Inspector Gadget…I don't freakin' know all right? All I know is that when she kissed me, I kissed her back. And before I knew it, I was picking up my eyeball. She got rocked too."

"What did you do?"

"What did you dew? What did you deeww?" Shawn said tauntingly.

"What do you think I did...? I did what you would not have. I got up, picked up the bat, and beat the crap outta him and his boys, till the police came."

"Did you go to jail?"

"No dumb ass. I ran. That is why I am in the den chillin' with a bowl of crunch, watching the tube."

Dad had just come home from work. I heard the door slam. It did not sound as if he were happy to be home.

"Shawn, Shawn, where are you...you little fuck?" My dad was yelling throughout the house. Before my brother could respond, my dad picked him up in the air and threw him against the wall. He had collared Shawn and drug him around the room. He then dropped Shawn on the same couch, where he had been watching television.

"Why are you so stupid? Why? Do you know that the police have cameras on the streetlights at every school? Guess what dumb ass, we saw the entire thing. I was so embarrassed, I did not even want to identify you. You almost killed them. Do you know that? You almost killed them boys. They are in the hospital right now fighting for their lives. I hope that they don't know your name, if they do, I can't help you son. I can't."

Shawn did not say anything. He just allowed the abuse to take place. Mom had heard the commotion and came down stairs.

"Eric, get off of him. Get off of him right now! What do you wanna do...kill him?" Tangie screamed as she got in between the two of them.

"Ask him where he was last night Tangie, ask him what he did!"

I ran upstairs and began to wash my hands. I washed them over and over again. When I finally felt that they were adequately cleaned, *about thirty minutes later*, I met my brother who had already been in sitting on my bed, playing with a switchblade that he kept under his pillow. He was twisting the blade into the palm of his hand. Blood began to trickle down his wrist. I didn't know what to do or say. I was scared for my brother. My eyes began to swell with tears. Don't ask me why but I had to ask...

"Shawn are you okay?" I whispered because I didn't want my dad to know I was talking to the enemy after he kicked his ass. Dad was good for asking someone else if they wanted a piece of what he was giving out.

Shawn didn't respond. He just let the tears run down his face and blood trickle down his wrist. We both sat there for a minute crying in silence. I asked him again...

"Are you okay, brobie?"

"I'll be okay, when he freakin dies. If he puts his fucking hands on me again, I will make mom a widow," Shawn replied. His eyes get wide and he begins to sob and hyperventilate uncontrollably. Now, I'm getting nervous. So I just start to look out of the window, hoping to find something out there to change the subject. But there was not, and my brother had more to say.

"I will get a fucking ax, and chop him up in his sleep. I will take off his arms, his legs, his hands, his feet. I won't stop bro. The cops will have to kill me. Then it will be just you and ma. I hope he gets shot in the fucking head."

I knew my brother was serious. If he thought he could get away with it, he would have killed dad. Now that scared the shit outta me. I had to sleep in the same room with a guy who got so mad, he wanted to chop his dad up.

I went to the dresser by the window and popped some pills. Although I was only supposed to take one, I really needed more tonight. As the pills took effect, I fell off into a dream state...

Chapter XVI

In a cold dreary cell, three persons await judgment…

In a world as cold and unforgiving as this one, it is always best to hold hands and stick together. That's what they were told and that's just what they did. They had no idea what to expect, but trusted the big boned enigma named Dot from the south, New Orleans to be exact. Dot did not come without a price. Her price was steep then, and it tripled after the disaster, but that did not stop the people from coming.

Before they traveled, Ms. Dot went over the rules….

1. "Do not speak, until I say."

2. "Do not lose concentration, stay close to me at all times."

3. "And do not, whatever you do…I repeat *do not* break the chain by letting go of anyone's hands."

"Do you both understand?" Ms. Dot said to them, as she said to all of her clients.

"We do," The James's replied. Although they had no idea to what degree that they were agreeing.

Most visitors, as did we, had to get a ride. There weren't many visitors who knew the way. The visitors had to find those who knew the way and then they had to be willing to take them. The ride was long and tedious. It actually seemed longer than life. *The courthouse was a long way from society, to say the least, but Dot knew the way.*

Just outside the courthouse, the sun geo-chemistrically, transformed the land into a scorching desert. For miles around its perimeter, there were no signs of vegetation. The fowl beasts were gliding in place above the campus awaiting the first sign of death. Outside the courthouse, just before entrance to the steps, stood two guards posted in front of the stone-carved gargoyles at the base of the steps turning away anyone who did not have proper identification. The gargoyles in their crouching position stood ten feet tall. They both had on identical "wife-beater" t-shirts. The top half of their uniform hung over the side of their shoulders. As people approached, they told raunchy jokes to each other and laughed as if they were the only ones outside.

"Excuuuse me. Do you think we would be able to enter the courthouse, it's freegin' hot out here," said one gentleman.

"Wait trespasser," one of the officers responded in a nasty tone without even looking in the gentleman's direction.

"Who does he think he's talking to?" the gentleman said. "Hello? Loogat this freegin' guy, telling jokes like he's Dice Clay. You've got people out here, whaddya thinking? We're sunbathing?" His conductor attempts to calm him down, but fails at the attempt. This guy was huge. About six foot six give or take an inch or two, and three hundred pounds worth of brazen strength as shown through his mannerisms. The officers noticed his stature as he stepped out of the crowd, but remained undisturbed. He boldly walked directly in between the two officers and poked one of them on the shoulders. As he began to speak, the other officer began chanting, "Viente a la vie. Viente a la Vie! VIENTE A LA VIE!" The earth began to quake. No one knew exactly what was happening. They were horrified. The gargoyles began to transform. It took a few minutes for them to awaken, but they came to life. Halfway through the transformation, he caught a clue and began to run. It was too late. The gargoyles reached consciousness before he was able to find his way home. They jumped off the pedestals and made a resounding screeching noise. Although they had wings, the gargoyles chased him down by foot, for the sport of it. The beast had claws. As it got closer to the man, the beast sprang up and sunk his claws into the man's calf impaling him to the desert floor. Blood spurted out of the man's leg. The beasts began to lick his leg. They loved the taste of blood. After the gargoyles tasted the blood, they encircled the man. The gargoyles positioned themselves at an angle of consumption. This angle finally allowed the people to be able to envision what had happened. The man was in a cocoon from his neck to his feet. The cocoon actually kept him living, but not for long. The gargoyles then picked him up by the legs, ripped them apart from the safety of the cocoon, and sucked the blood from his body until his eyes came through his feet. The crowd gasped in horror as they spat the eyes out into the audience.

It had happened many times before, but it only took the ghastly sight of one individual in the group to be helplessly devoured to bring peace to the masses.

Inside the courthouse, it was gray and cool. The holding cells resembled a prison, with the long corridors, and cells facing each other on each side of the corridor. There just outside of the wings, was a bubble (an office that was off limits to anyone except that officer), that had a type of blue tooth technology. The officer could activate the cell doors from the bubble without having to go to the rooms directly. From a piece embedded in his helmet, he could summon the goon squad to provide order in a state of disarray.

The air conditioning appeared to be overcompensating for the heat outside. The detainees overheard the guards talking to a man outside of the tier. It was not clear what was being said, however the floor officer said to the officer in the bubble open the "A" wing. The bubble officer opened the door. Footsteps could be heard from far away at the other end of the tier. The same tier that the detainees awaited trial. The footsteps became louder with every step. The detainees knew the footsteps of the different officers; this particular gait was not recognizable. As the sound became closer to the end of the tier, the detainees paced and reacted fiercely as if someone was invading their territory.

One particular detainee, named Demitri was planning an escape. Demitri had committed numerous felonies. He had a track record of devising wicked deeds, and malicious sorrow to inflict on others in his lifetime, and was not looking forward to his sentence. This strong willed spirit was determined to find the way out.

I'm gonna jump this fucker and escape this hellhole, Demitri thought to himself. He prepared himself for the escape. As the footsteps got a little closer, a strange feeling came over Demitri. When he finally got a peek at the so-called officer, he realized this person was not an officer at all. Sporting a high quality wool suit, as hot as it was outside, he appeared cool. This gentleman was tall, slender, and without blemish. He walked to the particular cell and waved his hand to the camera. The bubble officer saw him from that position and popped open the cell so that he could enter and chat with a prospective client.

"*Mr. Willie L. Barnsworth,*" the counselor said. There was no response. Mr. Barnsworth just looked at the man as if he had just seen a ghost.

I have come to represent you. Now time is short let us get down to business. I have looked over your file..." As the counselor discusses his case, Willie just looks at him in disgust. "*It seems that you are being charged with...*" and before the counselor could finish the statement, the Mr. Barnsworth responded...

"You? You are a niggra! Come back when your boss is available. I'm Willie L. Barnsworth, the L stands fo Lynch, and I won't have a niggra representin' me, he said with a screwed face. You got some nerves commin in her' and tryin' ta represent me!"

"*Sir, let's be clear. You are not going to accept my services because I am not white?*" The counselor continued to say, "*If I were a white person, would you accept my services?*"

"White, Jappaniggra, or Buddalicious-I can't afford it. So get outta here."

"*What if I told you that my fee is much better than what the other counselor is charging?*" the counselor rebutted.

"Get outta here niggra! What don't you understand about I am not payin' that I can help you with? *I wouldn't take* money to be represented by you! Spear-chuckin' is done outside of these her' gates! Now git...for I take off yur' tie and...hey where in da heck? You don't even have a tie on. Where is your tie?!"

"*I gave it to the judge,*" he said with pleasure. "*The judge did not have a tie and I let him borrow mine. It bought you some time, a reprise you could say,*" the counselor said with a smile.

"What does your generosity have to do with me? So you gave him a tie. You expect me to pay for it? I will take that damned tie off that judge and lynch you wit it Niggra, jus as sho as my name is Willie Lynch! Now git out and I mean it!"

"*As you wish, but about the tie...I wouldn't recommend it,*" the counselor said as he walked out peacefully.

The same counselor walked into the cell of Willie's wife. She began by stating, "*I have come to offer you council concerning your case, would accept representation from me?*"

Instantly she looked the counselor up and down like she had some deep-rooted ethnicity in her, and said, "You? A woman...You want to represent me? Do you know that my husband works at the United Nations? And they send me *you* to represent me?"

"*Ma'am, let's be clear. You are not going to accept my services because I am not a man?*" The counselor continued to say, "*If I were a man, would you accept my services?*"

"Male, female, transgender, chromosome reject! I don't give a damned!" I don't need someone like you, who can't help me."

"*Ma'am if I showed you my credentials and you were able to see for yourself that I have not lost a case would you still deny my services?*"

"That is probably because you never had one, who would hire a split leg to walk into a courtroom," she retorted. "Look at ya, you don't even have a belt on, but you consider yourself good enough to represent me. Ohh, I know where you left your belt...you left it in the council chambers. Under the desk where you'd been supplementin' your income, huh? I guess women lawyers really can make a *decent* livin'. Now really missy where in the hell is your belt?" Mrs. Barnsworth giggled.

"It is funny that you should ask. The bailiff needed a belt. So I gave it to him on your behalf. It bought you more time. A reprise if I may say," she said with a smile.

"Noo way sugar, I did not tell you to give anything away on my behalf. You spent that without my consent and you are out of that money on your own."

"I accept. So you are willing to accept my services?" the counselor asked once again.

"Nope," she responded. "Put your services where you put that belt. And put neither one of them on a bill for me."

"Well be that as it may, I did what I felt was in the best interest of my client." And again, she walked out peacefully.

Lastly, a small child is sitting Indian style-his face in the corner of the cold dreary cell. The young boy appears to be about four years in age, and clutching his heart with both hands. The cell is smaller than most of the cells on that wing, about half the size. He is alone in the cell, scared and sobbing uncontrollably. Even he, a young child is awaiting judgment. His own remorse does not allow him to notice the counselor upon entry, although the cell makes a loud noise, as it is popped open. The young child continues to recount repeatedly in his mind the deaths of his parents.

The counselor approached the child and realized that the young boy was aphasic secondary to the traumatic experience. The counselor assessed the young boy and found him to be an overstressed child no more than four years old. The counselor felt a certain sadness in his heart for the young boy and decided to take on the case pro bono.

The detainees were brought into the courtroom. They were all handcuffed with their hands in front of them. Although Demitri was at the front of the line, he was not the first to be called.

All rise for the honorable judge Luther...All had stood, except for the young child's counselor and his team, who had already been standing. In the front were many of the family members of the different detainees that were awaiting trial. Dot and The James's were as close as you could get to the trial without being a defendant. The James's were trying to locate their son. They saw him towards the back. However, he did not see his parents. When Mrs. James saw her son, she shouted to him. Dot squeezed her hand sternly, and that seemed to work for the speaking, but not for the concentration.

Mrs. Dot attempted to reach their son, Andrew; but Andrew could not hear her. The focus was not there. Someone was not in complete unison with the team. It was Mrs. James. Demitri caught the eye of Mrs. James. He used his influence to mesmerize her. It was a chilling connection. For Demitri, it was an opportunity. For Mrs. James an unwanted attraction. Both of the James' were losing all concerted efforts to travel. Mrs. James was being overcome by Demitri and Mr. James by his emotions of seeing his son again. Dot began to assist them. She repeated the rules...1. No speaking unless I say. 2. Do not lose concentration. 3. And most important do not release your grip. They began to refocus.

The dreary courtroom beautified with the old gothic marble, and even older legal staff. There were demon dog statues that were on both sides of the bench. There was also something foreboding about these statues. More foreboding than the others. These beasts transformed instantly upon summoning. They stood about six feet tall, but it wasn't the size that the people feared. These dogs were ferocious. They would rip into you, and torture you without opening up the gates of death. As you looked upon the bench, on the right hand side, you would see the bailiff. Strong, muscle bound, intimidating individual.

The judge sat on the bench, stern, obstinate, and unapproachable...

"Counselors plead your case," the judge stated attempting gingerly to remove his tie. The counselor of the defendant, Mr. Willie. L Barnsworth, asked his client to plead his case....

Chapter XVII

His Story...

The counselor began, "State your name."

"Willie Lynch Barnsworth."

"Where do you reside?"

"I live at 66-24 West End Ave. in Manhattan."

"Tell me in your own words what happened on the day in question," the counselor said.

"In my foolishness, I was unaware of what had been going on under my very own nose! I guess it had been a problem all along, but it all came to a head that one unforgettable day. The day that I actually caught my wife porkin' the neighbor!

One day...to get through it seemed as if it was a week...everything went in slow motion. I knew something was about to happen, don't ask me how...I just felt it in the depths of my soul. I woke up with the witch atop of me licking my face. I'm into that sort a thing so I just leaned back and enjoyed the show. She even licked my eyeball. That wasn't very cute. It actually grossed me out, the way she did it. It was too wet. She then straddled me as I lay on my back, and rode me for at least an hour. That hour seemed like the entire morning. I was exhausted. She got up and left me right there in bed, no kiss, no cuddle. I laid in the bed for a moment trying to figure out what just happened. I sat up, and wiped the cold outta my eyes. It was moist this morning, thanks to my wife's saliva. She licked me like a Saint Bernard.

Every time I took a breath, I felt this overwhelming need to exhale. It was a cold day, not as in the weather, but as in the spirit. Although she made me late for work, this particular morning, it did not seem to bother me. When I got up from the bed, I went to my son's room to see why he wasn't banging on our door at six in the morning like he normally would. The little bastard was scared to death. I tried to hug him but he just screamed and screamed. I left him there up under the covers where I found em'. I'm thinking to myself, what's his damned problem? I went to the bathroom to freshen up, I had ten minutes to get to work; of course, that wasn't happening. It took ten minutes to walk to the main road. I grabbed my face towel, lathered it well with some soap, and warshed my face. I cupped my hands to catch the water and threw it on my face a few times. When I cleaned it real good, I looked at it. I was horrified. My eye looked like it belonged on something else's face. A thing that eats people. I rushed to my wife and said, what in the hell is this? The sewer rat never even looked up at me..."

"I object," the prosecutor responded.

But Willie continued louder, "she just pretended she was asleep under the covers. How could she be asleep and the porch monkey screamin' like he ain't had no damned sense...Sometimes I'd wonder if the little bastard was mine."

"I object your honor the counselor said in exasperation."

"Sustained," replied the judge.

"But that is their nicknames, or at least what I call'em," Mr. Barnsworth said in defense of his earlier comment.

"That's not my damned nickname!" His wife yells in rebuttal. As she was defending her character, she had a seizure. The seizure had her flopping around on the floor like a fish getting tazered. She tried desperately to control the seizure. Mentally however, she was shackled. She was able to tell her body what she wanted done, but somewhere in between the synapse, the connection was lost. Her body would not cooperate. She realized then, she had no control of her body. With her eyes bulging out of her head, and saliva drooling out of her mouth, she was terrified. Not one person in the courtroom moved to assist her. .. especially not her husband. As she attempted to recover, the Judge said to her...

"Young lady in my courtroom we do not act out as you have done. I suggest you have more respect for the justice system."

She could not respond. It was as if she was still recovering from the seizure.

"May I continue?" Inquired Willie.

The judge sneered at Mr. Barnsworth, and then he just waved his hand as if to say he could continue, although it seemed he was not interested in what Mr.

Barnsworth had to say. Mr. Barnsworth continued cautiously in the beginning, but then became comfortable once again.

"When she finally awoke from her comatose state…kinda like how she is looking right now (she appears to be postictal), she grabs the first thing she can get her hands on your honor and knocks the crap outta me. Normally, I would have ducked, but my eye was so heavy, I could not move my head fast enough. She hit me square in the good eye your honor with the expensive bottle of scotch. I could not see at all. I ran around the bedroom, smashing anything that came my way. When I finally got to her, I slapped her around good, and she gave it right back to me. She ran downstairs into the kitchen, and I slammed the bedroom door, and locked it. I knew she was going for the kitchen utensils. I finished getting ready for work and left through the balcony exit. I guess she had forgotten all about me, because she knew how to open the door if she really wanted to. She was busy trying to feed the little rug rat and send him off to school."

"I object your honor…the boy is not a rug rat!" The counselor stated in defense of the child.

"Sustained," said the judge.

"Well the little monster that does not pay rent! As I was going to the pick up point, I saw her bringing him to the school bus. Just before getting on to the main road, I saw my neighbor. The limo had been waiting there. It was 8:30 in the morning; my neighbor was cutting his lawn, waving at me, and smiling all too pleasant.

'Good morning neighbor,' he said.

'What's so good about it?' I responded, rubbing my eye and I jumping into the limo.

'Whoa! Dude, what happened to your eye?' The neighbor said as he stopped the limo driver from closing my door.

'That witch hit me with a bottle,' I said.

'You should put some ice on that eye, what was in the bottle? A bee's nest?' he responded jokingly, still keeping the limo door open. At this time my wife walks past us in a very sexy manner, they exchange greetings, and she goes on towards the house. He was a fool to think I did not see him lookin' at ma wife, the way he did. I was even more of a fool not to think nothin' of it. As he continued a conversation of irrelevance, the damned limo driver began to act like my boss.

'You're approximately one-hour late sir, and I took the liberty to contact Mr. Frost, we have to leave,' Charlie said.

'That wasn't necessary, Charles,' I responded. It was quiet for a moment, an uncomfortable quietness. I knew he wanted to say more, I just did not want to hear it. He finally got the words together and said, 'You are going to have to be on time, because it is a reflection on me as well as it is you, Mr. Barnsworth,' as if I were working for him.

'I would rather walk to work than drive with you!' I told Charles.

'And I would rather drive over a cliff than take you to the United Nations building,' he grunted as he kicked me out of the limo."

"I object your honor," the prosecutor said. "The limo driver stated that he refused to accept a ride from him."

"Is the limo driver here now?" The judge requested.

"He was, but he regained consciousness. He cannot travel here in his present state. I do have his testimony however, and can play it back."

"It is not admissible in this courtroom. Continue," the judge gruffed.

"So I arrived at the annex in Manhattan. I paid the cabdriver, got my briefcase out of the back seat, and ran into a crowded elevator. As I got off the elevator and entered the lobby area of our floor, my boss was pointing at his watch, as he eyed me through the glass partition. I received the full affect his anger through the pane. After a brief preparation in my office, I hustled to the meeting. I was supposed to present a mock treaty to the representatives of the different nations. I had a strange feeling that came over me.

'Whoa, dude what happened to your face? That doesn't look good at all. Are you sick?' One of my peers said aloud as I tried to present.

'I am coming down with something,' I responded, thinking that would end that conversation, but of course it did not.

'Is it contagious? I think you had better go see a doctor for that,' another peer added.

I was really hot. I was sweating in places I did not even know I had glands. I could not finish the meeting. I had to return home. Not only because I had felt sick, but because my boss was being anal. He released me for the day. Furthermore, I just knew something was wrong in my home. I got a voucher and took a limo home at once. When I finally got to the main street, I tipped that limo driver and walked to my house. I heard music coming from my bedroom. I wondered to myself, why is this hag playing this music so loudly? Something told me to look in the window, to see what was going on. Although I saw nothing strange, I was compelled, by a force not of my own, to continue my investigation. I went around to the south side of the home, and climbed the stairs to the second floor terrace. I had the terrace specially built when we first got married. It was a hobby for my wife to plant flowers and this gave her an outlet while I was at work. Little did I know she already had an outlet. The terrace connected to the balcony, and the balcony opened an entrance to our master bedroom. As I passed the terrace, I heard strange noises coming from my bedroom. The closer I got to the balcony door, the more nauseous I became. It was my wife. She didn't sound like she was being attacked...well not any way that was disturbing to her. It disturbed the heck outta me though. I peeked through the glass door of my balcony leading to my bedroom. The whore always left that sliding door open. The only thing camouflaging me from her sight was their intense indulgence in infidelity. Her and the neighbor had been boinking the entire time I went to work; and from the looks of it, she left her panties at the front door, cause they were no where to be found at the site of sin. He was pawing my wife and making sick stomach aching love to her. My wife was on top of him, straddling him as he lay on his back. In my favorite position...IN MYYY BED! At that point, I was enraged. The neighbor however was more alert. He cautiously pushed her off of him, and reached for his pants. By that time, it was too late. I was all over him. My wife ran outta the bedroom. Taking over my wife's position, I grabbed his naked ass by the neck and looked in his face. My God, his eye looked like he had already been in a fight. Man, did it look terrible. It would not stop the chokehold I placed on him. I choked him good...to his death; or so I thought. Then I dragged him back to his house and through him over the fence. I returned to my house and interrogated the harlot. She ran into the kitchen. I was directly behind her, not letting her get away from my wrath. I grabbed her by her shoulders and asked her why? She laughed at me. It hurt. I would not be laughed at in my own home. I would not be disrespected again by her. I slapped her face. Hard. She looked up at me with her evil eyes, and spat in my face. It felt like battery acid. She laughed a second time. That was a time too many. Although I could not see, I felt my way to her neck and pressed against it. As I squeezed the life out of her, she continued to look right at me with that sick, you can kill me, but you can't hurt me face. I forced her into the wall unit and broke the glass where the fine china was stored. She kicked me in the privates. Without answering the rhetorical question, she started scrambling in the drawers for a knife. She got the butcher knife...I tried to get it away from her. She stabbed me in the guts. The blow would have killed me if I were a weaker man. I managed to get the knife, but not after it had slashed her face and nicked her throat. We continued to fight and bleed. She ran upstairs into the bedroom. Although it was still difficult for me to see anything clearly, I was right behind her.

The school bus had honked. That meant the little brat was coming home from school. It was at this time that the neighbor's wife came out of the home. She would normally get the kid if we were not able to pick him up. She would then bring him to her home and fix him something to eat. After she fed him, she would call one of us on the cell to make sure we knew where he was. She did the same thing this day, except as she was walking back to her house she found her husband sprawled out near the lawn mower. She started screaming, ran into the house and called the ambulance. Leaving the little monster to run home alone.

Why the little guy came home early I never understood, but he found the trail of blood by the staircase. He followed the pool of blood directly up the stairs and into the bedroom. He saw us bleeding like pigs in a slaughterhouse, and got scared…I told him to come to me and his mother told him to run as if I was going to hurt him. 'Call 911,' she said. What did he do? He ran. He ran as if his life depended on it. He did not get far though, he ran right into his room and got under the covers.

I was tired, and so was she. We both fainted. I don't know why. Maybe the excitement, maybe the lack of blood, maybe the infection. Whatever the reason, we were slept like someone slipped us a benadryl cocktail. I woke up before her and placed her in bed. As she lay naked under her robe, I had a psychotic lust within me saying, make love to her. I had to succumb. She woke up to me inside of her. She stared blankly at me on top of her. Seeing that I had tamed the beast, I collapsed on top of her. It appeared to me that she had let this thing be reconciled. As she lay conquered, I returned to sleep. When I woke up, I was in a cell waiting for my court date."

Chapter XVIII

Her Story...

The counselor began, "State your name."

"Janice Kathlyn Barnsworth."

"Where do you reside?"

"I live at 66-24 West End Ave. in Manhattan."

"Tell me in your own words what happened on the day in question," he said.

"Your honor, there was something in the air that day. I don't know what it was, but I just did not feel like myself. I woke up early, about six o'clock in the morning. I may have rested in the bed for about ten minutes, and then decided to get ready for the day. I went into the bathroom and freshened up. I took a nice warm shower, and was actually feeling ok at that point. I went outside to the balcony air, and took a deep breath. I was trying to smell my azaleas, but the air was very stale. Each time I took a deep breath, I had to cough something fierce. I was coming down with something. I knew it was not lady like to spit, but I had to get this mucosal growth out of my mouth. I walked to the terrace and spat in the soil. The soil seemed to be bubblin'. I thought to myself, *I have got too much bug killer in the garden.* I tried to smell the different flowers that I planted in the garden, but could not smell a single one. I began to feel really hot and bothered. There was a sinister breeze blowing, but I did not feel cool at all. I began to perspire. I thought that maybe I was coming down with the flu."

Her counselor interrupts her, "Mrs. Barnsworth could you start at the beginning and tell us why you are here today?"

"Yes. I would like to say for the record, that I have never slept with anyone but my husband."

"May I remind you Mrs. Barnsworth that you are still on oath?" The judge said to her.

"I know what I am saying your honor! Now if I *may* continue," she reported matter-of-factly. "I got up very early this particular morning as I always do to shower and smell my flowers on the terrace, before I start my day. Normally, after the floral rejuvenation, I would start breakfast, but I decided to give my partner a treat that he didn't appreciate!"

"Partner, who me? HA! The neighbor was your friggin' boink partner!" Willie yells out of turn.

At that moment, Mr. Barnsworth gave the universal choke sign. Willie suffered a respiratory attack. His airway closed up and he could not breathe. He sprawled out on the ground trying to force air into his mouth. Approximately a minute passed by before he finally recovered. When the air finally hit his lungs, it was insatiable to him. He continued to deep breathe and hold his chest.

"I have zero tolerance for disrespect," the judge stated. He furthermore stated, I will now make myself *very* clear. He attempted to remove his tie once again, it had loosened but it would not be doffed.

"Bailiff!" The judge growled.

The bailiff began to adjust his belt. Instantly within the blink of an eye...no long transformation...no hocus pocus...the devil dogs came to life. These flesh-eating monsters flexed their superiority by surfing the courtroom. Their speed was unsurpassable. These spirit-clenching monsters had teeth that could eat through bone like scissors sheared loose-leaf paper. They continued prancing around the courtroom directly causing terror in the hearts of men and obediently waiting for a directive to strike. They directly bestowed order to a captivated audience.

One of the dogs snapped at Mrs. James. Instead of Mrs. James clutching tighter to her husband, she let go of his hand completely. Dot felt the disconnection and shouted, "Hold his hand quickly! Hold his hand!" Mrs. James finally complied, but it was too late.

"Continue Mrs. Barnsworth," the judge stated in a reassuring tone.

"So when I went down stairs to make breakfast your honor, my husband just sat up in the bed, like he was not going to work. What am I going to do? I made breakfast for my boy, and we ate. Here he comes rushin' now because he was late for work, trying to blame me. His eye was lookin' something terrible. I just laughed because he was scaring tha baby. He did not like me laughing at him, so he started to smack me around. I fought back with all I knew how. I ran up the stairs, and he grabbed me and forced me onto the bed. I turned around, picked up the scotch bottle, and knocked him square in the eye. He fell out. I ran downstairs, got my boy, and took him off to the bus stop before the bastard could retaliate. Here he came, your honor right behind me. The only thing that stopped him from beating the crap outta me in the street was the neighbor. He stopped the slime ball, and asked him some questions. I thanked the neighbor. It seemed like he understood what I was going through all too well. The limo came to pick up Willie about the same time the school bus came. The neighbor stopped the limo, to speak a little more to my husband, which gave me time to slip by the psycho unaccosted. I returned to the house, gathered the dirty clothes to put in the warsh. After taking care of the warsh, I then began to hang the wet clothes outside on the porch. I was still in my nightgown at the time I was hanging the clothes, which I felt was okay, because I was not going anywhere special, and I was on my own property.

The neighbor saw me hanging the clothes and came over to ask me if I was feeling ok. We talked for a moment, and he realized that he needed some fertilizer for his wife's garden. So we went to the back to get the fertilizer and foolishly, we tracked it through the house...it was a short cut to the front door, and closer to his home. Of course you know fertilizer is heavy and you don't want to be carrying it a long ways. The fertilizer spilled on his overalls and got him all dirtied up. So since I was doing the warsh, I told him that I would clean his overalls also. As soon as that man got his overalls off, I went to the bedroom to get him something else to wear. I was sure Willie wouldn't mind letting him borrow some sweats and a shirt while his was in the warsh. When I get into the bedroom the neighbor follows me in uninvited. He turns up the music loudly so he cannot be heard. He grabs my shoulders and throws me onto the bed. I am fighting him off of me, but he easily overcame me, in more ways than one. I spat in his face. This stunned him and I was able to get on top of him. My jealous husband came through the balcony door. At first I was relieved, but I saw the red in his eyes. I ran into the kitchen. He began to wrestle with the neighbor. He choked the neighbor to death, and drug the neighbor outside...I guess to bury him. At this point, I was terrified. I just knew that when he returned he would seek to kill me too. I prepared my defense in the kitchen. When he entered, I grabbed a carving knife. He charged me your honor and fell onto the knife. It had no effect. He continued to be a wild man. He grabbed the knife and cut me twice. The first cut was the deepest...he slashed my throat from one side to the other. I bled. I became delirious. I saw my life flash before me, and lost it. I ran upstairs to the bedroom. He was right behind me. As we continued to fight, my son walked in from outta nowhere. That bastard told my son to come here. He was gonna kill us all. I told my son to run...run like your life depended on it and call 911 like we practiced! My son did just that. My husband dragged me to our bedroom and still with weapon in hand, had his way with me. I was violated until he fell asleep. I quickly grabbed the knife and finished him off while he was sleeping. I felt my life leaving me also. I called my son back into the bedroom. I kissed him. After that, I blacked out.

There was no response from the judge or the jury. The courtroom was in disbelief. The devil dogs were just feet away from her; taking turns snapping at her like a starving pack of wolves to a piece of adipocerous carnage.

Chapter XIX

The window of life…

We have time for one more testimony.

The Counselor responds for his client. "*Spawn of Satan, we will testify through the window of life because my client is mute…*"

Everyone in the courtroom gasps in horror. As the window of life enters the courtroom, it is not a window at all, well at least the windows to which they were familiar. It was a continuous sphere. The globe changed in size until the view was conspicuous and visible to all. The globe was placed in testimony to reveal the truth. Not only the truth displayed in the child's mind, but the truth that was embedded in all of the participants mind's that were involved throughout the entire day. It also focused on the child's reoccurring tribulations. The truth was going to be told, although it had a challenge seeing the light in this courtroom.

The globe envisioned…

The globe began the testimony by projecting the morning of the day in question. It is five o'clock in the morning. In each room as the globe narrates, all the Barnsworth's were asleep. The first to see the morning was Mrs. Barnsworth. She had been awakened by a strange wind at the balcony door. Although the curtains muffled the sound, she had an inclination to what she thought it was. The natural ear was not able to discern that the sound was a demon. She went to the balcony to receive a full charge of the breeze. The demon rushed into her airway. To her surprise, the breeze was stale. She began to cough, unaware that her spirit was trying to exorcise the demon from her body. Her spirit failed.

She closed the balcony door, and walked into the bathroom. She peeled off her nightgown and stepped into the shower. The water was warm to the touch. After the shower, she brushed her teeth. As she spat, she noticed that her excretion was red and frothy. She rinsed her mouth and looked at her tongue; it was also red. It began to develop small growths...growths that appeared to secrete that frothy, reddened substance that came from her mouth earlier. She was clearly sick. She ventured outside to receive a second dose of that stale air. She was hot, perspiring at the brow. It was early in the morning. The sun was trying to make its way through the clouds. She felt a pasty collection in her throat again and relieved herself of it in the garden.

She returned to the bedroom where her husband was sleeping. She began to wake him up. He was still drunk from the previous night. She licked his toes, not for the fetish, nor for the passion, but for the excretion of the substance on her tongue. She continued all the way up his body until she got to his face. She then licked his eyeball, and that was all he could take of the licking. He did accept the rest of her love gestures, and she loved him for a long time. He laid flat on his back, receiving without a balanced giving. Mrs. Barnsworth relieved her itch, and coldly left him sprawled out nakedly in the bedroom. She went downstairs and began the breakfast.

Mr. Barnsworth did not want to get up, but was happy his wife left. He was exhausted. He had a fifth of scotch by the bed, Mr. Barnsworth grabbed the bottle and he sucked it down until there was just a corner left. In his drunken stupor, he realizes that he was going to be late for work. He places the bottle aside, and rushes to his son's room, and lift's him in the air. The father's eye along with his excitement was too much for the little one to bear. He became frightened, and began to cry uncontrollably. Mr. Barnsworth not understanding the reasons behind his son's reaction became upset. He threw the boy on the bed and stormed out to return to his bedroom, again, not realizing that the boy was terrified by the eye. He went into his bathroom, and began to lather his face. With his hands, he loosened the mucous that closed his eye. When he rinsed his face, he saw his eye. He ran down the stairs and snatched up his wife, who was in the kitchen making breakfast. He said to her, "What in the hell is this on my face?" She responded with laughter, which infuriated Mr. Barnsworth. Mr. Barnsworth fought his wife often, but he would never hit her in the face. He did not want the tabloids to get a hold of an abuse story. This time however must have been different. He slapped her once across the face; she just looked at him in disbelief. He smacked her again, she snarled with laughter, but she was by no means enjoying the punishment. She spat in his face, and then ran upstairs to the bedroom. He ran after her. She tried to close the door, but he was right behind her and challenged the attempt. He burst through the door, which had thrown her onto the bed. She grabbed the first thing that she could which was the scotch bottle and let him have it. She caught him square in the other eye. He cried out like a child scorched by boiling water. As he held his eye, she ran downstairs to the kitchen and grabbed a sharp kitchen utensil. He got to the bedroom door and locked it. He then went to the bathroom and looked at his eyes. He whimpered a bit more and continued to prepare himself for work, by this time he was clearly late.

Not wanting to feel the steel she kept in her hand, he went to work, exiting through the back door. As he was leaving, she prepared her son for school. She and the boy walked out right after him. No one said a word to the other, although they were walking in the same direction. She still carried the utensil in her hand, and the child in the other.

The neighbor stopped mowing his lawn to say hello to the parties. They acknowledged his greeting. Seeing Mr. Barnsworth's eye the neighbor came out of his yard to speak with Mr. Barnsworth. They arrived at the main road, and Mr. Barnsworth was getting into his limo. This did not seem to deter the neighbor at all. He continued to ask Mr. Barnsworth questions about his face.

Just at that time, Janice was returning from taking her child to the school bus. She passed by the neighbor talking to her husband and gestured for him to come by later. Although the neighbor saw the gesture, no one else did. She also gestured that she was going to put the knife she was carrying in his neck. He also saw that gesture, no one else did.

Mr. Barnsworth got into the limo. Having been late already, the limo driver gently explained that he needed to interrupt their conversation because they were late and he had to leave immediately. He was ignored. They spent five more minutes talking. The limo driver again getting out of the car, said it again, this time a bit more firmly as he helped the passenger door come to a close.

Mr. Barnsworth complained about the embarrassment he felt by being rushed, as they were driving down the street. He stated that he did not ever want Charles to tell him what to do again, attempting to force Charles into a promise. When Charles refused, explaining that he did not work for him, he worked for Mr. Frost and Mr. Frost wanted everyone at work on time…Mr. Barnsworth began to scream at the top of his lungs, and called Mr. Charlie all kinds of racial insults. Mr. Charlie stopped the car and called the office. Mr. Barnsworth used a few more choice words and walked out of the car.

The next vision was back at the house. Mrs. Barnsworth had been completing the laundry, and hanging the laundry outside. The neighbor watched her hang the clothes as he mowed his lawn. She again, gestured for him to come over. This time he accepted. As the neighbor's wife slept in the house, he walked over to the Barnsworth's home and gave Mrs. Barnsworth a hug. He did not stop with the hug. A cordial hug became a passionate hug. The neighbor then gave Mrs. Barnsworth a kiss. The kiss began with the lips...then included his tongue. She returned hers. She began inside his mouth. She licked his face, and slid her tongue to the outside of his ear. She even licked the organs inside his ear. Again, not for erotica, nor for the fetish, but to get the mucous out of her mouth. It was nasty, but he liked it.

He could not see the evil she had bestowed upon him. All he knew was that he was turned on. There were no more clothes to hang on the line, and Mrs. Barnsworth had fulfilled her need, although he had not. As she returned to her home, he asked could he borrow some fertilizer for his wife. She knew he did not need any fertilizer, but did not challenge his request. She allowed him to get the fertilizer, which was in the back of the shed. She allowed him to go through the house. It was a faster route. There was no need to venture to the bedroom, but she went, and he followed. He turned on the music...loudly. Unbeknownst to him, he had become deaf in one ear. The same ear that was pleasured by Mrs. Barnsworth. The neighbor could no longer take Mrs. Barnsworth's teasing. Her gestures along with the pleasantries, as she walked around in nothing but a nightgown, turned him on. But her tongue action and the way she licked on his ear...it maddened him. He took a chance, and grabbed her close. The phone rang. He never heard it. Although she heard the phone, it was never answered. It was the school wanting to say they were returning the child home because he appeared too ill. They left the message on the answering machine and called Mr. Barnsworth on his cellular.

The neighbor had thrown Mrs. Barnsworth onto the bed and sucked upon her supple breasts. Mrs. Barnsworth allowed him to use her body to pleasure himself. She then turned him over and began to pleasure herself by licking his salty skin. Again, Mrs. Barnsworth was found to have violated someone's wedding vows.

The next vision is a drunk Willie, finally getting to the office, because he walked out of the limo. When he got to the lobby of his office. Mr. Frost was staring at him through the glass. Still being drunk, he walked into his office and began to prepare the presentation. Mr. Frost burst in and said, 'you have nerve...real nerve talking to Charles like that. He works for me and I asked him to make sure you are here on time so if you have a problem it is with me, not Charles. I expect you in the conference room in ten minutes ready to present.' Mr. Frost left. Mr. Barnsworth received a phone call. It was from the school. He told the school to send the boy home. His mother would be there to pick him up. He then hurried into the meeting and began to speak. Before he could get well into the presentation, someone said, "Good Lord look at your face!" still another peer stated, "Man your eyes...I think you better go home." Mr. Frost gets a good look at him, and says your eyes are blood shot red, and as he walks closer, he smells liquor on his breath. He sent him to the clinic to get a blood sample. Mr. Barnsworth never went to the clinic as he was asked. Instead, he took a voucher from the receptionist, got a limo service driver, and went home.

The next vision is the limo driver letting him out just at the main road. He walked the rest of the way home. Approaching the house, he heard some music. Mr. Barnsworth first went to the front door, and peeked through the window. He was going blind, and could not see the keyhole. He went around to the back of his home through the garden and on to the balcony. He knew that his wife always left the balcony door open. As he got to the balcony door, he witnessed his wife and his neighbor having sex in his bed. The loud music...his wife giving away his love...his neighbor accepting the love, he went into a rage. His wife saw him at the door, and rushed to get up. The neighbor not knowing what the problem was began to look for his pants. It was too late. Mr. Barnsworth was all over him.

He choked his neighbor almost to death. He thought the neighbor was dead so he threw him over the fence near the lawn mower. It was clear he tried to make it look as if the neighbor had a heat stroke mowing the lawn. It was also clear that there was another spirit there, a spirit that no one else could see.

The next vision happened to be the neighbor as she was picking up the child, and returning with him to her home. The child had been coughing. She began to look for her husband, so he could run to the store for the boy's medication. She found her husband collapsed in the grass, as the lawn mower was still running. The neighbor screams in horror as she ran into the house to call the ambulance. Frightened by what he had just witnessed, the little boy ran straight into his home.

The next vision was the Barnsworth's as they fought in the kitchen. The little boy was in the corner peeking at the entire scene. Willie charged his wife and the wife stabbed him with the butcher knife in the abdomen. He managed to take the knife from her and sliced her twice. He slashed her once on the right side clear to the left side of her neck, and again on the right side of her face. She, as well as he was bleeding like a slaughtered pig. She ran to her bedroom, leaving a trail of blood behind. That same trail of blood was used to track her down, although he could not see very well, he was close enough to her to follow the sounds. He couldn't grab her because of the blood on the floor made him slip up the stairs. He could smell the diseased odor of her blood. It kept him energized. He challenged her at the bedroom door again. The little boy screamed, "Please don't kill mommy! Daddyyyyyy!" That was the last words he ever uttered. Mr. Barnsworth got the door open and threw her upon the bed. The little boy followed his father. He had also slipped on the blood earlier as it was on his hands and cheek. He watched the entire scene, without one tear. He appeared to be in shock. His parents saw him at the door. The father was going to kill him. He asked the boy to come over to him. The mother felt murder in his voice and told the boy to run and call the cops, her voice was hoarse and could not be heard, because it was damaged by the ailment. The boy received the message of her eyes though. He ran into his room, closed the door, and crawled under the bed. It was also clear that there was another spirit there, a spirit that no one else could see.

The next vision is of the Barnsworth's in the bedroom making passionate love. No one being violated, both welcome participants. In the end, they both fall asleep. When the wife awoke, the son had gone back into the bedroom and sat next to his parents Indian style on the floor. The wife stabbed the husband in his back, taking his life. The child witnesses the entire slaughter. She called him toward her. He came. He was guarded upon his approach. She gave him a hug, bleeding all over him. She then stabbed the child directly through his heart. As his life left, so did hers. It was clear that there was another spirit present, a spirit that no one else could see.

The last vision is the police on the scene to this bloody mess. They question the neighbors. The neighbor was taken away in the ambulance. He was later arrested for more questioning. He was caught lying to the police regarding his whereabouts.

Just as that scene is finished, Mrs. Barnsworth stated, "Your honor I took my child's life so that he would be free. I also took my own life, so I could be free. It seems like the wrong thing now...but at the time it was the only thing that I thought I could do. Can you understand this? I did not want my son to live in any foster home! I guess I just went psycho!" Mrs. Barnsworth spills out desperately.

Almost simultaneously, Mr. Barnsworth states, "That thing is lying, I was not gonna kill my child! I love that little boy!"

The Counselor of the young boy states, *"the evidence speaks for itself. We request that the court accept the plea of innocent, no adjournment for my client is necessary, he has been forgiven of all wrongdoing."*

"I am the ultimate decision maker in this courtroom and I say the court will adjourn," said the Judge.

The court adjourned....

When the judge returned, The Counselor, and the little boy were gone. The judge had the tie loose but it was still around the neck as he attempted frantically to remove it as a courthouse prisoner trying to remove handcuffs. The bailiff had been trying furiously to get the belt off. He finally got it unbuckled. When they finally removed the unwelcome accessories of clothing, they metamorphized.

Dot not only knew the way to the courthouse, she also knew the way home, and when it was time to go...it was time to go. She escorted her clients home before it got ugly. Little did they know, they had an unexpected hitchhiker. Demitri was loose. He had entered the soul of Mr. James when the devil dogs frightened Mrs. James into breaking the chain. Although they were safe at home before the courts could render a decision, as long as Demitri possessed Mr. James, they were nowhere near safety.

"The court has rendered a decision," the judge spoke aloud. At this time, the scales of justice turned into skull and crossbones. The bailiff threw away the belt and transformed into a demonized dragon and the judge finally took off the tie and with a horrific laugh, transformed into the infamous Satan. He howled, "I sentence all of you present to burn in the sea of eternal Hell!"

Chapter XX

When I woke from the nightmare, I was still in my clothes. The clock had struck midnight. I ran out of the condo, and into the hallway to see if the lights were still flickering. They were. Oddly, it made me feel safer. As long as the lights were flickering, I knew that Sirius was nearby. I sat in the hallway for a bit to share my thoughts with Sirius.

"I do not get it, why am I the one troubled with these nightmares? And how are they helping you?" I asked.

That would take time to understand…and that you don't have much of. You have been resting a long time, but you are in need of some more sleep. You will need all of the energy you can muster for the final dream. It will take a lot out of you. I hope you are prepared to handle it.

"*He* will not give me more than I can handle," I responded with one of those clichés that was so familiar among my congregation.

We will see.

The lights discontinue flickering, and Roman returns to the condo. He goes upstairs, pops some pills and returns to bed for a restful sleep. As he slept, his mind drifted into a vision.

Chapter XXI

Revelations 13:4

People worship the dragon because he hath given his power to the beast. And they also worshipped the beast, asking, who is like the beast? Who can make war against it? The Revelation...

Every thirty-four years, on a certain date, the most intelligent of the unforgiven get a second chance. The gates of Hell open up and the worst of the damned shall contaminate the earth...

In hell...

"I will free three spirits," the demon said in a commanding voice. The sea of souls instantly became restless. Out of the billions and trillions of souls, only three had he requested. The souls had a better chance trying to ice skate atop of molten lava, but it was a chance. The souls were thirsty, to say the least. Of course, the Devil knew that action would cause chaos. And it did. As the demon souls were fighting amongst themselves, there were four souls trying to find out when the portal would open. These souls had no intention of fighting for the three slots available. They were determined, and had been determined long before the request of the beast, that they would make their escape.

There were four select spirits, Subvidious, Anglore, Tempest, and Curmis.

Subvidious. This intellectual genius used his cerebral superiority to hustle grandmasters out of their money on the chessboard. Also, being a mind walker, he could at times listen to what his opponent was thinking, and in that way have an advantage over an otherwise even game. It was written, *the love of money is the route of all evil.* Subvidious allowed his greed to get the best of him. Subvidious died a slow and painful death…it all went awry on one consequential day at the hall.

At the under ground gambling hall…

As the song played, *you never count your winnings while you're sitting at the table, they'll be time enough to count em' when the dealin's done!* Subvidious walked in as he normally did, with an indirect gait…a gait of impaired neurological functioning. He circled the joint, approximately one or two times, looking for his partner, Fritz. Fritz, or Vaquero, his alias in the gambling halls, was already at the tables. They made eye contact, but no greetings were exchanged. Subvidious hovered at the tables about one or two minutes, then ended his scout at the bar.

"Hey Craven," the bartender said to Subvidious. Craven was the name he used in the circuit. "What can I get ya?" Heaven said with a smile. This sexy virago stood about five foot ten inches tall. Her hair was short, with tight curls on the right side and around to the back. On her left side, the hair was straight, but cut in a slant, and covered her almond shaped eye when she wanted it to. It was dark with light colored blends in it, matching her darkened complexion. Physically, her body fit the description of what most people thought Heaven should be like…although most people she encountered would never get to know the truth.

"How about a Mental House?" He said smiling right back at her.

"Coming right up," she said, brushing the hair away from her eyes.

The chess table opened up…Craven tipped Heaven more than she deserved and took his drink to the board. It had just so happened that Vaquero was at the other end of the board. As they played, Vaquero was telepathically speaking to Craven. He told Craven that the money was on the poker table, and they could probably leave the hall with fifteen thousand between the both of them. They would just have to locate a victim. Make sure he was alone. Allow him to win, along with them, and we will rob him as he makes his way home. It was a great plan; they just had to make sure that no one knew that they are together.

Scanning the room for the victim, they found that there were two minds that they could not read. This set up a red flag. It meant that there were other mind walkers in the hall or there were people who had encountered mind walkers before and discovered a blocking technique. Either way, the feeling was uncomfortable. Vaquero decided to abort the plan. Craven tried telepathically to talk him out of it.

"It's only two. Two on two is a fair fight, they are probably in here doing the same thing we are…trying to pay their rent. Craven thought to Vaquero. After the two talked it out, they found their victim. It was a young drunkard at the end of the

bar. He was boisterous, with plenty of money. A perfect combination. Craven walked over to him and began a conversation.

"Hey partner, can I buy you a drink?" asked Craven.

"Long as I don't have to be your girlfriend...sure," he responded.

"What's your name buckaroo?" Craven said trying to make small talk.

"Daniels, but they call me.. Cain," he said as he failed to think of something cooler.

"Well Cain...do you do?"

"Sometimes, I am a professional gambler, when that doesn't work, I am a professional lover, when I can't make a livin' on that then I am a professional beggar. I guess today, I am a gambler," he said as he flashed his money about.

"So you are...So you are." Craven was mesmerized by the flashing of money.

"What do you do?" Cain returned.

"I guess you would say I am a detective. I take on cases..." before he could describe his falsified occupation, Cain responds, "I know whatin' the hell a detective does!" and he began to laugh.

"What in the hell is so funny?" Craven said.

"What do you think? You come in a place like this and the first thing outta your mouth is that you are a detective. You're special," Cain said as he takes his brew to the head.

"I know...but listen I just came in here to supplement my income. I know that you are pretty good," said Craven.

"How do you know?" Cain replied sarcastically.

"I'm a detective," he responded, this time almost believing it himself.

"Oh yeah, I almost forgot. You want me to play with you...what's in it for me?"

"We'll split everything fifty-fifty."

"Not good enough," Cain burped.

They continued negotiations as Vaquero scoped out the tables. He had been pacing the floor for a while, not trying to get in, but just looking to see where the money was at and where the weakest link was seated. He found them both at the same table. It was too good to be true. He signaled Craven to hurry up. They both caught the signal.

"Look our table is ready. I made you an offer and you refused. What is it gonna take for us to make money?"

"A sixty-forty cut. Majority goes to the professional. I think that is more than fair."

"I accept. Come on, there is an opening at table twelve," Craven said as he grabbed Cain out of his chair.

They were playing straight poker at the table, no chaser. There were two partners already at the table, one of them being Vaquero and another victim. They were willing to play with one more pair. Since the table was open, they walked right into the game. They sat down and Vaquero was giving the play by play to Craven through telepathy. Craven and Cain continued to win their pots. Cain had been boasting about his winnings. Upsetting the other players.

"Can I get you boys a drink?" Heaven said, as she stood over the table. She took the orders, although she already knew what most of them were going to order. They ordered the regulars, and she had returned with them quickly. Cain made small talk as he slipped something in Craven's drink. As soon as Craven took one sip, he felt something was not quite right. He sucked it down though, and she bought him another before he could wipe his lips. He started to lose a hand or two. Cain was not worried, but Vaquero was. Vaquero mentally spoke to Craven, but it seemed as if Craven was not listening. Vaquero realized something was wrong. Craven would not just ignore him like that. He guessed that Craven had put down one too many, and was not able to focus. Then Vaquero started talking in crypt on the board. Instantly, it was picked up by Cain, and he pulled his weapon.

"If I'm gonna get whooped, it's gonna be fair and square, now the way I sees it somebody owes me this here pot," Cain said

"Whoa big fella, slow down. No one's cheating here," Vaquero said as he gets up in defense, Craven followed suit.

"You think I would do something ignorant like that? Trust me man I got better sense than that," Vaquero stated.

"Why should I when you are sitting here in my face talking the board? I am losing money and I am gonna take it outta someone's ass!" Cain yelled. At that moment, Heaven returns with another round of drinks.

"Come on daddy, don't make me have to take the shit starter from ya, it would be embarrassing. Can you let me be a lady tonight?" Heaven said as she rubbed his chest. "Come on daddy, this drink is on the house," she said with a smile, as she said everything. Her voice could calm two male pits fighting over a monogamous bitch. He did not take her seriously...about the taking of the shit starter; they called it the shit starter because every time someone pulled one out, that is just what it did. She talked him down, but she was not scared to get it on with the best of them. Many of the players already knew that she was serious, and even though all of her pearly whites were on display, she meant every word that she said. The last time someone pulled out a shit starter, she took the weapon, kicked his ass, and shot him in it on his way out.

That broke up the game. Cain had already split up the money, and was ready to leave.

"Thanks for the big day detective. We have got to do this again," Cain said jokingly.

"No prob. Thanks for taking me on. Hey are you going towards Cheyenne?" Craven asked.

"Sure am, but I ain't driving, so if you're looking for a ride you'd better get one of the other boys," Cain responded.

Vaquero is trying his best to interact in some way with Craven, but Craven could not hear him. As Cain leaves, Vaquero walks up to him...

"What's your problem? You have to pay attention! We could have been killed!" Vaquero whispered.

"Fritz, I mean Vaquero...I did not know you were talking to me. I couldn't hear anything you said."

"That's because you were drunk! That was stupid. We lost out on a great deal of money. Let's go!" They finish their drinks and Craven goes to the bathroom before they leave. The two guys that had been blocking their thoughts walked into the bathroom right behind him. They stood there and stared at him as he was using the open stall. He knew something was strange, but he could not place his finger on it, and too drunk to attempt to figure it out.

They had been making sure he could not hear telepathic transmission. A mind walker, unknown to Vaquero, spoke to him through mind transmission, saying that Cain was going to Cheyenne and he was walking...hurry up and follow him. I will catch up to you later. Not remembering that there could be other mind walkers in the bar, he thought he was speaking to Craven. He also thought that Craven was sobering up. He finished his drink and searched for Cain.

As Vaquero approached Cheyenne, he saw Cain walking towards the North side. Vaquero followed him.

Craven finally got out of the bathroom, and looked for Vaquero. Of course, he could not find him. Craven then sat back down at the chess tables with the money that he had won. In a matter of hours, he was broke and the hall was about to close. He could not even buy a drink, and he really needed one.

"Craven, last call...I'm ready to go home," Heaven said. She was tired. This had been a good day for the owner, which meant it was also a good day for her. She cleaned up in tips tonight, more than usual. She felt as if she worked for every penny though. "You wanna earn a drink and a tip tonight?" Heaven asked.

"Whaddo I gotta do?" He replied, knowing all to well that she could have asked him to do almost anything, give or take the almost, and he would have done it, just to see her smile.

"All you gotta do is walk me to the car. It's a few blocks down the street though."

"Sure honey. You know what I'm drinkin'." She mixes his drink. After fixing the drink, she goes to the back to count out her register.

"Get down! Get down and don't make any mistakes...I guarantee I'll make it your last!" A gunman taunted.

Heaven heard the commotion outside. She used her cell phone to call the cops. She assured that the entrance to the safe room was locked. She sat in the middle of the room, Indian style and began to search for the Being inside her.

Since the place is being raided, Craven decides to get into the other register, while the place is being robbed. He puts on his ski mask and goes for the register. All of the unlucky players that were left behind, observe Craven as he jumps the counter, and steals the money.

The robbers filled their bags with the wallets and trinkets of the left behind players. Their greed was unmatched. Although they had taken all that was in their vicinity, they wanted more. Two of them went to the safe room door. After unsuccessful attempts, they finally broke the door down with brute strength.

As they entered, Heaven met them in the center of the room, but she offered no resistance. Instead, she continued to sit quietly Indian style, and in intense meditation. She was outside of her body looking at the entire scene.

The robbers knew her and knew of her skills. They would not be caught off guard, their weapons were drawn and they were ready. With her eyes being closed, they assumed that she could not see. They assumed wrong. She saw what they could not see.

"Open the safe!"

She did not respond, nor did she move a single muscle. All of her energy was focused. On what, no one knew. It seemed as if she was in a deep sleep. They could have probably cracked the safe themselves, and left her to meditate. Unfortunately, that was not what they did.

"I said open the damn safe bitch, I know you hear me," the first robber said.

"Just kill her, we don't have time for this shit...I bet the cops are coming right now!"

He shot the weapon. The bullet traveled so fast, that it appeared to glide through the air in slow motion. As the bullet approached, Heaven, returned to her body. She shifted her left shoulder up and brought the right one down on a slant. Immediately, like a ninja perfecting the Harlem shake, leaned back away from the bullet, as it ricocheted off her medallion. The bullet flew into the light fixture; as a result, the entire room was dark. Except for the tips of the weapon, when they were being discharged. The robbers could not see farther than their hand in front of them. Heaven could see what was happening and what was going to happen. She had light; therefore, she had sight. Her light lit the room, but it only benefited her sight. And she used her sight like a sniper. Although they continued to spray the entire room and the contents of the room were riddled with bullets, they were not effective. No other bullet ever came as close to Heaven as the first. As the bullets continued to fly, Heaven advanced. Her approach was as delicate as her beauty, and far more deadly. She slid her hands upon the first robber's weapon, and turned it upon him and unloaded on his kneecaps. As the first robber screamed in agony, the second discharged his weapon in that direction. He did not care who he hit as long as he caught Heaven. After falling onto his injured kneecaps, Heaven snapped his neck and used the remains to shield against the shots fired in their direction. The second robber decided that he was satisfied with the money he had. He forgot about the safe and attempted an escape. Heaven crawled along the walls in an attempt to block his exit. He made it to the street, with the help of his weapon. He discharged another weapon as he ran, but again missing at each attempt to splatter her brains against the gambling hall walls. The police had arrived and upon witnessing his escape, he was shot and killed as fled the place.

Craven was long gone at the time the cops arrived. Halfway down the street, he takes off his mask and heads north, towards Cheyenne. He saw Cain, and Craven saw him. Cain walked towards Craven, and Craven backed up as if he knew that something was not right. He backed up into the other two goons that shared the bathroom with him earlier. Craven ran down an alley where he saw Vaquero…sprawled out with his eyes wide open. He was murdered in cold blood. It must've been a horrible death, Craven said to himself. He began to hear telepathic communication. It had been loud and sinister.

Not as horrible as yours will be detective. At that moment, he knew that they were set up by mindwalkers. *Some freakin' detective you are. Hahaha.* He continued to laugh until his stomach tightened. *Oooohhhh my that's funny. Maybe you can figure this one out.* At this point, the jovial laughter transforms into a sneer as he communicated telepathically. *It's pretty easy. Why do they call me Cain?* Craven, knowing he is about to die a slow and painful death answered as he turned around slowly to face his assassins, *because you murdered your brother.*

Chapter XXII

Anglore, another lost soul, experienced the first half of the natural as an adored changeling, and the other half as an ostracized scoundrel. In a changeling's culture, a name was of great importance. They would be identified by their sir name and the title from their profession. This was a changeling's full name. Those changelings, who did not have a career, were just called by their sir name. This was unacceptable in their culture. An adult changeling needed a professional name to attach to their sir name.

Anglore was born of a wealthy family. It was once said in an ancient proverb, *it is harder for a rich man to get through the eye of a needle, than for him to get into heaven.* But Anglore was not a man. He and his family were well-respected changelings from the planet Zandor. The Anglore clan desired a high priest in their family. Many were chosen, but none could answer the call. None until Anglore himself was chosen. High priests, as with all leaders of a religion, had to live virtuously first, before any other tests of worthiness. After, they had to prove excellence in physical fitness. This consisted of a restricted diet and rigorous training regimen. They had to be masters of the martial arts. There were many long days of training. Anglore's chambers were upon the mountains away from the followers, as all were housed training to be spiritual leaders. He and the other students would leave the chambers before the sun arose, and would return long after the sun went down. They also had to have spiritual fortitude. This required deep meditation, prayer, and mental discipline. The latter was particularly important for the second half of the challenge of high priesthood. This was also the greatest challenge for Anglore. Anglore trained long and hard. Harder than was required, if it was even possible.

High priests of Zandor trained all of the time. Many could not complete the journey. The ones who did were treated with the respect that exceeded that of a baron.

Every high priest expected to read and memorize the Sacred Scrolls. It was written in Zandori, their ancient language. Although archaic, it was still understood and almost exclusively utilized by the high priests. Some were able to read the ancient language, but this still did not permit access to the Sacred Scrolls as they were hidden in the sacred mountain. Where no one of unclean mind and body was allowed to enter.

The Chief High Priest Zillus gave his blessings upon the commencement of *The Rituals of Advancement.* This ceremony was treated like a holiday. The students trained many years to reach this pinnacle of their studies. The ceremony of the rituals lasted for two days. Family members and friends of the family would come from near and far to witness the occasion. After the two-day event, most would have five days to rest before returning to work. The families would take their children home, away from the sacred mountain. This meant a break for the families that presented their sons and daughters to God to join the priesthood. They were not allowed to visit their children on the mountain. The mountain was sacred ground, and was only treaded upon by the spiritual leaders and their students. The exception to this rule was during the ceremonials. It was a happy time for all. The students knew that during their recess they were going to break their diets. Mothers would prepare their favorite meals. Although they were young, they would be allowed to partake of the top shelf liquors and the finest aged wine. There was no legal age limit to drinking on Zandor. The fathers would test their children's martial arts. Neither male nor female was treated any differently when it came to the lessons in the priesthood. Even combat, as the females fought just as well as the males. In some cases, even better.

Anglore's family was very proud, because he took home many weaponry and martial arts awards. There were others who received awards, but it was different for Anglore, because the odds were against him. His ancestors had never reached the point to be recognized in ceremony. They had always been expelled, or surrendered before the event.

After the festivities, it was time to return to the mountain. This was difficult for Anglore. He was in great shape physically, but the spiritual aspect of the teachings were lacking. He did not fully understand his spiritual path. When he would, it would be too late.

Anglore was alluring. He could bring many to the path of righteousness. His style was comforting. The same style that benefited the craft also caused his demise. Anglore was a young man in the age of a changeling. His youth, although it helped, it showed his inexperience in the spirit. Anglore was very intelligent. He just lacked the nourishment. Therefore, he lacked wisdom. The deep-seated wisdom that his peers had and that he was expected to have, eluded him. He would not heed the advice of his mentors willingly. It was only after embarrassing mistakes, that he would concede, and receive the teachings.

It was written that a special high priest would come receive the knowledge to read the secrets of the cave. These were hieroglyphics chiseled upon the plates and walls of the underground chambers.

Changelings believed there would come one who could read the secrets. No one chosen thus far had received that sight. The students that performed well in the last event during *the Rituals of Advancement* were asked to become high priests. This is also a great honor, but this time it is private. No one other than Chief High Priest Zillus was allowed to test the student. After the exam, no one was to know your scores, not even your other peers. If a student did not pass the examination, he or she could not stay. If a student passed the exam, but was not orally and literally fluent in the ancient tongue, he or she could not stay. If they could not use the secrets of the scrolls, they had to return to the teachings, and search for the answers they could not find previously. Lastly, if a student did not accept the charge of a high priest, they could not stay. This was a serious charge. They did not make the ceremony public for that very reason. They wanted a true acceptance, with the pure heart and mind. Not a heart or mind tarnished by the influences of the unclean spirit.

A bonus given to the students of the ritual included the attempt of the secrets of the cave. Anglore had finally received his opportunity. Now it was time. He attempted to read the secrets, but could not. His pride forced him to emote the shame he felt. He was given time alone to express his malcontent.

Anglore was asked if he wanted to continue with the end of the ceremony. He accepted and recommenced his calling to the path of righteousness. He took the oath, dedicated himself to the craft, and was ordained a high priest of Zandor. He was now entitled, High Priest (HP) Anglore.

As a newly ordained high priest, you were awarded with an amulet. This amulet was of treated titanium. It was the created to be the strongest metal known to a changeling. There were metals similar, but nothing this strong, or this metallic. It was made to be a distinguishing feature of the high priests. It showed all who came upon you that you were of the cloth. Wearing this amulet, you were expected to be a demon slayer. This amulet was formed in the shape of the Sacred Scrolls, and it had a sapphire to represent the seal of the Scroll.

There were tasks that newly ordained high priests had to complete, many of them menial. The highest honor for a newly ordained high priest was to guard the Sacred Scrolls. This calling was only given to the few who attained the highest honors during the martial arts segment of *the Rituals of Advancement.* It was given to HP Anglore. This honor was only given to him once. It proved to be the only time that he or anyone else for that matter, was given the revered task of guarding the Sacred Scrolls.

The first night, HPAnglore protected the Sacred Scrolls. His uniform was crisp and clean. His mind was fresh. It was apparent that he was honored. He continued to protect the Sacred Scrolls for that first week. He was comfortable in the role that was given to him. It was a task set aside for the student who proved to be the best martial artist, and one that could be trusted.

The last night of his lawful watch of the Sacred Scrolls, he began to think about the secrets of the cave. The exam that he failed began to replay in his mind, and again he was ashamed. Ashamed that he, along with all the others that attempted could not read the secrets. He then looked at the Scrolls. He stared into the glass case that protected the Scrolls. There must have been a clue in the Scrolls...a clue that he did not catch. He needed to decipher the secrets of the cave. There must have been something within the writing of the Sacred Scrolls, because the memorization was not helpful unlocking the secrets of the cave. Since he had the key, he knew that he could open the glass case and delicately remove the scrolls. That was just what he did. He tried very hard to decipher the scrolls. He read the scrolls and stared at the cave. Nothing. The night was leaving, and the early morning coming upon him. He had become possessed. HP Anglore could not return the scrolls. He concealed them in his robe.

As he attempted to leave, the sentinel who was guarding the entrance attempted to stop him. Not expecting that HP Anglore had been an enemy, he did not sound the alarm. That mistake was fatal. HP Anglore deactivated the alarm with his weapon. The high priest fought fiercely for ten minutes. Ten minutes that seemed like an hour, but HP Anglore's skill easily evidenced to the sentinel that he was untouchable. HP Anglore was practicing his art as his counterpart was fighting for his life. As the high priest became aware that he was losing, he tried to escape. He crawled sideways against the wall attempting to evade his attacker, and exit the foyer. HP Anglore had predicted his escape and closed all the doors and windows using his mental abilities. Propelled by a stealthy glide, HP Anglore removed the pathway of escape from the sentinel. As

HP Anglore took flight, he again confronted his victim with a flurry of blows. After the sentinel recovered from the fists of fury, his response was a counter assault from the air. The air assault proved futile, as the sentinel was returned back into the wall unit that show cased weaponry. The sentinel was finally hurt. He tried desperately to use his voice as an alternative method of alarm, but HP Anglore grabbed him by his jugular. He looked at HP Anglore in a bewildered state, just as HP Anglore looked at him as he whispered, "I am ending your life so you can die with dignity." HP Anglore then murdered the high priest in cold sacred martial art blood. No one ever knew the truth, and it hurt too much to suspect. In the early morning they found the high priest, he was laying in a pool of blood. There was no trace of HP Anglore.

The Sacred Scrolls were a curse to him. Word of the Sacred Scrolls traveled quickly. HP Anglore tried to sell them. No one would buy them. The high priesthood was hunting down anyone who they thought was responsible for the murders of the high priests and the removal of the Sacred Scrolls. Therefore, he who possessed The Sacred Scrolls was forever in danger.

HP Anglore survived as a nomad underground prizefighter. He would mutate into the specifications of a fight. Changelings did this all the time; it was not illegal. What was illegal was killing a high priest. Not only in this life, but in the afterlife as he soon found out. He eventually buried the scrolls in an undisclosed location and ended his own life, because no being in any arena was fit enough to end it for him.

Chapter XXIII

Tempest another lost young soul, was a very bitter child. A child that never asked for a second chance in life. By grace, she was given a clean slate to return to the natural from a failed previous life. A life where her evil deeds were forgiven. However, since she did not learn the lessons of life, to life is where she returned. This was where the second journey began...

They say that all children go to heaven, in Tempest's case this was a sick lie...

Her spirit was evil from the womb. Tempest was carried for nine months. That in itself was the only normal episode of the pregnancy. During the last six months, soon after the first trimester, the pregnancy became turbulent. The mother was having severe cramps; she went to the emergency room three times a week, thinking she was having a miscarriage. Although her doctor conducted a battery of tests, she could not find the trouble. The doctor placed her on bed rest. After the seventh month, the pain became unbearable. Her husband asked her to think about abortion, but she would not even entertain the request. Not to mention, it was rather late in the pregnancy. The mother knew something was wrong, she never had this much pain in her life. It was soon time to deliver the baby. Early morning on June 6, 2006, Tempest was born. Her mother died soon after giving birth to Tempest. She died with a smile on her face, the purest smile Tempest ever brought to anyone's life thereafter. It may have been the only one.

Ten years later in Public School 206...

Sharon was a schoolmate of Tempest. Sharon, larger than most of the children in her class, was clearly outstanding. She had a sweet clumsiness about her. A clumsiness that was noticeable, but not alienating. She was taller, heavier, and most importantly, had a bigger heart. She always received awards for most helpful, and most friendly. Although very humble, she prided her amicability. These attributes were innate in her, as with all of her siblings. The teacher allowed the class to go to recess, except for Tempest. Tempest was being punished for chanting in the classroom while they were taking a test. When Tempest was finally allowed to return to her class, they only had fifteen minutes left to play in the schoolyard. As Tempest pulled her hair back, to fix her ponytail, Sharon ran to her, displaying her new doll.

"Hi Tempest, look what I got for Christmas!" Sharon exclaimed to Tempest after returning to school from the winter break.

"You got it for Christmas? Wow, let me see it!" Tempest grabbed the doll and danced around, as if the girl had given it to her. "Can I have it?" Tempest asked.

The girl thought about it, never forgetting how volatile Tempest could be when she did not get her way, she replied, "Tempest, my mom gave this to me for Christmas." Young Sharon didn't know that Tempest's mother died giving birth to her. It was the worst response that Sharon could have given.

"YOUR MOM GAVE IT TO YOU?" Tempest inquired, waiting for any verisimilitudinous response or even a sign of such.

Sharon nodded.

Tempest then bit the head off clean off the doll. Then she flung the doll as far away from the little girl as her arms could manage. Tempest then said as she pushed the little girl to the floor, "NOW SHOW THIS TO YOUR MAMA AND TELL HER TEMPEST DID IT!" The teacher blew the whistle one time, which meant that you had five more minutes to play. Tempest left Sharon on the floor and returned to enjoy the last few minutes of recess.

Young Sharon was hurt. Not hurt because she had been injured, because she really had not been...not physically anyway. Neither was it because of her doll. Although it was a collector's edition, she knew that she could get another if she just asked her mother. She was disturbed about the doll, sure, but not hurt. What hurt her was Tempest's actions toward her as she was the only person that would befriend Tempest. Sharon just did not understand. Young Sharon remembered her mother saying to her that she could get along with anyone if she tried hard. She really wanted to be a friend to Tempest. For her it would have been an accomplishment, for Tempest it was another attempt to destroy the good in a person.

Having more insight than given credit, she never told the teacher, because she knew that the teacher could not control Tempest. It would just make for a long, hard day. She did return home later that day and tell her mother exactly what had taken place.

Sharon's mother, Mrs. Grant, usually very amicable, was not at all pleased with Tempest's behavior. It showed in the phone call that was received by Mr. Payton, Tempest's father. Sharon's mother then called Mr. Payton and retold the story that Sharon had explained. Her voice was stern. She wanted to hear that Mr. Payton was going to handle this situation for her daughter.

"…Mr. Payton, one more thing before I end my phone call. The doll that she ruined was a collector's item…I am not asking you to replace the doll, although any responsible parent would have already offered to do so, but I do believe that your daughter owes mine an apology."

"I hear you Mrs. Grant, I will talk to my daughter, and we will work this thing out, I assure you that your doll will be replaced. How much was it?"

"Three hundred and fifty-nine dollars," she said without blinking an eye.

"Holy shit! Three hundred and fifty dollars? Why'd she take *that* one to school?!" Mr. Payton screamed. Mrs. Grant sighed in exasperation and hung up the phone.

Mr. Payton endeavored to change his daughter's heart on many occasions. Being a NYPD detective, he even tried tough love. He confiscated the handful of things that seemed to bring enjoyment in her life. He had removed items from her room until just a dresser remained to keep her clothing. He was at the end of his rope. He confronted Tempest. Tempest never denied it; she just ignored her father as she went to the fridge to get a cold beverage. He loved her, and told her this, but his anger was evident.

"Tempest I need you to stop walking away and listen to me," he said. When that did not work, he grabbed her. She just looked at him. He yielded. Tempest stepped out of the kitchen gracefully, as she felt her battle had been won. She went into the living room, where the only television to which she could gain access was being neglected. He, not wanting to be defeated, rushed into the living room, and slapped her across the face, "Gat Dammit, Tempest…you are gonna listen to me! You killed your mother and you sending me to my deathbed! What in the hell is wrong with you?" Mr. Payton execrated as he shook her one good time. She did not move or even release her stare. One tear fell down her face. It was the only sign that she was crying. She did not appear to feel the blow. She did not even appear to feel.

There was going to be some tougher love in this house. What the father failed to realize, was there was also going to be some tougher hate.

That night she did not eat. Neither did he. He did have a drink though, about a fifth of brandy. He needed to erase that evening of being out of control. Soon after the last corner of the bottle was finished, he showered and went to bed. Although he erased the memories of the evening, Tempest had been replaying the entire episode back in her mind, repeatedly.

Tempest waited until her father was sonorously asleep. She went into the kitchen and grabbed the cooking oil, and a lighter. She trolled to the bedroom in a spellbound state. Tempest witnessed the apparition of her mother in the bedroom window. Her mother had not aged at all. Her pureness captured Tempest's cold heart. Tempest stared at her mother strangely for a moment. It lasted just long enough for the spirit to bring a warning. She endeavored to expiate the birth of Tempest with her warning.

Tempest's mother spoke to her husband. He could sense her presence with every sense known to him, but only through his dreams.

You have to get up now! She warned.

"I love you, and I miss you," he said her, ignoring her plea.

You must wake up! Again, she warns.

"I slapped Tempest, she has become a demon child, Honey, I failed us...I am so sorry," he mumbles as he attempts to wipe what his dreams lead him to believe are tears from his eyes. The liquor had him shackled to his dream state. He was happy to see his wife as he smiled in his sleep.

Tempest continued to pour the cooking oil over his face as he wiped it off. She then emptied the bottle on his body and mattress while he slumbered. She then got some bleach, ammonia and anything else she could find to ascertain that she would send him to his wife first class. She lit the head of the doll, and threw it on the bed. She went to the closet and appropriated his firearm.

The fire burned quickly and spread fast. He got up horrified; instead of stop drop and roll, he panicked. He got up and tried to grab Tempest. Tempest shot him, but he still did not die. She ran all over the house. He ran behind her releasing a terrifying shrill, "TEMPEST...WHYYY!" The scream of death, echoed in the walls of the home, it even echoed throughout the entire neighborhood. He chased her until his legs burned off his body. He was a strong man. His eyes and his voice were engraved in her mind as he burned to ashes. Tempest succeeded her quest in sending her father to the other side. When he finally gave up the ghost, Tempest looked at her mother's spirit in the window. Her mother placed her hands over her face, as she could not take the horrifying experience.

The NYFD team of emergency workers came; they were not able to gain access. They had reported a child in the front of the home brandishing a weapon. That child was Tempest. The police came with their weapons drawn, but not with the mind set to use them. That was their mistake. After trying to talk her down, one officer, Eric Phoenix, stepped passed the other officer's to speak with the child. He told her it would be okay as he walked towards her to accept the weapon. She gave it to him...shot him directly in the head. Split another officer's Adam's apple. He eventually died after being sent to the hospital. She killed two of them and split another officer's wig, before the police finally sent her home. One shot to the torso. She did not pass go did not collect two hundred dollars...she went straight to hell.

Chapter XIV

The last lost soul was Curmis. Curmis died a serial killer. He graduated from Aviation High school. Twenty-four years young, Curmis was about to graduate from Queens College.

His stress level was beyond functioning levels for a long time. He did not know the warning sign's, nor did he know how to relieve stress when it was finally detected. Curmis did not have a girlfriend. Pressure can burst pipes. It had also burst one's control of sanity as experienced in Curmis' life.

Playing basketball his first year of high school, Curmis befriended a jock named Damion. They met at practice in Flushing Meadows Park. All of the teams trained there because it was huge, and convenient for most of them. Although Damion was not big at all, he was fast. He played football and lettered in his first year. Damion was good. He never earned a full scholarship to go to college. The college scouts blamed it on his size. Damion eventually went to a community college somewhere in Long Island City, and never played the sport again. Curmis lost touch with Damion. They both took different paths in college.

One day while Damion was jogging in Flushing Meadows Park with his girlfriend, Curmis had recognized him. They hugged and talked, far exceeding the ten-minute time limit set in his girlfriend's mind. She taller than Damion, an athletic, rather attractive buxom woman, began to show her annoyance.

"Curmis, this is my girl…Chris," Damion said to be polite.

"Hi, nice to meet you," Curmis said extending his hand.

She shook his hand gently, smiled her return greeting, then she quickly faded out as they began talking.

"What are you doing with yourself now? I thought you would be playing for the New York Giants around this time!" Curmis said.

"Yeah, they did not see me as a Giant though. They told me I had a better chance playing for a team called the midgets," he joked.

They chatted about the old times, the girls they dated, and what ever happened to people they knew. The minutes turned into a half an hour. As Chris continued jogging in place, she became increasingly annoyed. She hummed and hawed, trying to throw Damion a clue, but she never spoke a word. She just looked at Damion with those eyes like, hello…let's go! Damion, seeing the anger in her eyes, told Curmis that they had to go, but for Curmis to call him, "we'll hang out," he said as they exchanged numbers with their pocket technology. She then tugged him away from the conversation.

Later that same night they talked on the phone. It was as if they never lost contact with each other. One night became two, and before it could be subdued, they were hanging out in clubs together. They became better friends than they were in high school. They drank, almost every night. Curmis began to miss a few of his early morning classes. The finals were upon him. During that time, he failed every exam that he took. Although he was devastated, he knew this would be his consequence. His judgment was poor…his insight was better, but not by much.

Damion's girlfriend was getting pretty tired of the cold shoulder she had been getting from her soon to be X. Damion began to talk negatively about his girlfriend, as they got drunk in the club. Eventually the question was asked.

"Damion, does your girl have any friends?"

"Naaah, man, she doesn't hang around anyone that I would introduce you to."

"What do you mean?" Curmis asked.

"I mean…they're all crabs," he said as he started to imitate a lobster.

"Whoa," Curmis responded monotonically.

"Yeah man, they all look like Lou…" then he started singing, *You'll never find…a chick with a mind. Someone who is down for you…and go down on you.*

As they laughed, and talked, Curmis seemed to have forgotten the finals he blew this semester.

When Damion got home, he was met with poison. His girlfriend had given him an ultimatum.

"Either he straighten up and fly right, or you can call Tyrone, or what ever the freakin' guys name is you're dealing with and he can help you pack."

"Baby, relax. You're overreacting to the situation. I haven't seen that guy in years. He's like my best friend."

"I'm your best friend! Got it?! I am your fucking best friend!" She says looking for any sign of disloyalty. "I bet you he doesn't know anything about you," she says in a voice as deep as his own. She looks at him in disgust and walks away.

Chris enters the club, with a few of her friends, none of them being female.

Chris walks into the bathroom as Damion is micturating. He feels someone looking at him and he turns around...

"Chris what are you doing in here...dressed like that?" Chris had dressed in hip-hop attire.

"I think it's time I spoke with your little boyfriend," Chris said.

"Come on Chris...what in the hell are you talking about?"

"You know exactly what I am talking about," she said as she pulled out her penis, flopped the flaccid beast around, and traveled in a bumblebee pattern to the nearest urinal.

"God No! Chris this is not the time. Is this why you wanted to hang out? To hurt me? I am begging you not to do this to me. I love you Chris." Just then, a man walks out of one of the stalls and looks at them strangely.

"What you never seen homosexuals in New York City? POOF, GO AWAY!" Chris screams as he makes gestures of go away with his hands. The patron, very embarrassed, walks out the bathroom without washing his hands.

"If you don't want me to make an ass of us both, then you have to show me you love me, instead of just saying it when it is convenient for you...I need you to show me right now!"

Meanwhile, about three stiff drinks later, Curmis had been wondering what was taking Damion so long in the bathroom. He didn't want to leave the drinks unattended, but he also knew that Damion's drink was no longer fresh, as the ice had melted. He noticed a group of people by the bathroom, and decided that he would investigate.

Curmis staggered into the bathroom and heads straight for the urinal, to return a derivative of what he drank at the bar. He noticed there were two people in the stalls. He also heard Chris making a feminine sex noise.

Curmis says, "Hey Dame, is that you in there?" He got no response. Just then, one of the guys waiting outside the bathroom for Chris, walked into the bathroom. He didn't say anything; he just scoped the place out. Curmis, now a bit more than tipsy, put himself closer to the urinal, as he suspected someone spying his organ.

The guy noticed his protected stance and walked to the adjacent urinal. He looked Curmis directly in the eye, scanned him up and down, then breathed quickly, "humph!" snubbing Curmis. Curmis not realizing he was outnumbered, responds, "Just because you keep a dick in your mouth doesn't make you a urinal, now stop staring, freakin' penis ogler!"

Chris burst out of the stall and came to his friend's defense. Damion stayed behind. Curmis does not recognize Chris at first, but Chris recognized him. Chris called his friends into the bathroom. Having just enough sense to know there was about to be a problem, Curmis tried to leave. They do not allow him a pathway of exit. Curmis finally realized that he was on the wrong side of town, at the wrong bar. He wondered to himself, why Damion took him to *this* place. As he recollected, he remembered that the reception upon their entry was not very friendly. He also recollected that there were not many women, especially any that had shown an interest in him. He then turns to Chris, and eyes him through the thuggish clothing. He said, "Do I know you?"

"Yeah duke, I'm Chris...Chris to...fucking...furr!" He growled as he sprayed his face with a stream of saliva from the annunciation. At that point Curmis realized, he was not just a homo...he was a homo-thug. "What was that you said about a dick in my man's mouf?"

Curmis clammed up. He had enough soberism to know he could not beat them all, and they were heated about the way he expressed his revelation. He could not even scream, the house music was at ear bleeding levels, not that it ever crossed his mind.

Before he could bring understanding to the thugs, they rushed him. As one of the thugs kept the entrance door closed, the others beat him up and forced him into the last stall. Damion knew what was taking place. Although he knew everyone in the bathroom, he chose not to takes sides. He remained in the stall and locked the door.

Curmis was entered anally by the entire crew, except of course, Damion. Although Damion wanted some of the action, he did not want it like this. Damion wanted to help his friend, but knew that if he did, there would be two victims instead of one. Dame was a coward. And he knew it. He was ashamed by his lack of backbone, but could not do anything about it. The tears swelled in the wells of his eyes, but he somehow stopped them before they could come streaming down his face. He felt very sick and alone.

After they had their way with Curmis, Chris called out to Damion. Again, Damion did not respond. Chris would not call a second time. He jumped over the stall and unlocked it. Chris opened the door. He pulled Damion out of the stall, and directed him to Curmis's stall. Curmis was curled up around the toilet bowl, with his pants hanging about his calves, bloodied and worn. Damion and a beat up, violated Curmis locked eyes upon each other. Curmis realized that he trusted the wrong person to have his back…Damion. Damion forced his way out of the bathroom. The homo-thugs followed behind. Chris was the last person to leave the restroom, smiling in a satiated manner.

Curmis, violated by a crew of homo thugs, went crazy. He said to himself they are gonna wish that they never knew me. He became a nemesis. Eventually he murdered every member of the crew.

That was not what sent him to hell…he received so much pleasure spilling blood, he did not end the spilling with the thugs. He spent a great majority of his time traveling. He would hitchhike along the highway, and anyone who would pick him up would become a victim. He loved the look of a man just before he was going to die. It was like a drug to him. The drug that caused his demise. Every time he killed someone, he would allow them to see his face. He would then say those infamous words…"I wish you heaven, because I am going to hell." He did not lie. The sad part is that Curmis began this journey just fulfilling a vendetta, but the smell of blood and fear sealed his destiny.

When the spirits entered the portal, they had no idea where they were going or what they were going to do. However, they only had a matter of seconds to find out. The spirits could not live outside of a source for longer than a minute. After one minute without a source they were forced directly back to hell.

Anglore went into a commanding officer. Unfortunately for Anglore, he had chosen the wrong body to snatch. The officer had been in a perilous situation, a few minutes before certain death. Subvidious went into a chess game. Usually you were not allowed to inhabit a non-living object, but an exception was made as long as someone or something living was occupying the board, or a game was in session. Curmis went into an airborne virus. The last who was Tempest, went into a lady on her deathbed.

Chapter XXV

At the home the night before the hospital…

Janice drove into the parking lot that evening hot and exhausted. She didn't have enough energy to get out of her brand new toy, the hot pink convertible Volvo, given to her as a gift. She always drove her prized possession to special events. It was one of the biggest jobs she had ever done. Orchestrating a dinner for approximately five hundred members. The day went just as she expected, long, and unbearable. The members of the executive team were very demanding. They ran her team around like hunting dogs.

She waited in the car listening to her CD's until she could muster up enough energy to wipe the sweat dripping from her thigh. She had been blaring Maroon Five, Sunday Morning. *'Fingers trace your every outline ohheeyea, paint a picture with my hands'*. She opened the car door, placed both of her legs out on the drivers side as if she were getting out but didn't. She began to massage her long slender legs. She began at the thighs as close to the hips as she could manage, one leg at a time. Irritated by her tight, wet underclothing digging into her skin, she slides off her panties, and continues the manual massage. Laterally and medially, her hands in motion simultaneously, she sensuously manipulated the large muscles, first in a large ovular motion. She then continued at the calves, only this time she appeared more detailed. Her oval motion concentrated on each epithelial cell. She crossed her legs. One leg at a time, she massaged her ankles, right ankle first. With her eyes closed, she took off her pump and began gently rubbing the ball of her foot with her thumb. She then imagined taking a long hot shower. She then changed to her left ankle and repeated the process evenly.

She entered the home with panties, pumps, and purse in hand. She turned on the air, and peeled off the rest of her professional clothes. She went directly into the bathroom. She sat on the edge of the tub naked. Her smooth silky skin gently pressed against the ceramics with her legs crossed towards the head of the shower. She allows her dominant arm to stabilize her body as she solicits her other hand to adjust the water. The water gushed from faucet hard, cold and fast, but her hand remains in the water faithfully until the stream of frigidity abates.

As the temperature of the water began to satisfy, she felt relaxed. The sensation of warm water traveled from her hands throughout her entire body. It cooled off her hot naked body. She collected her toiletries and stepped into the shower. She lathered her hair and applied the body wash as she normally would after a long hard day. As she showered, she heard music playing from outside the bathroom. She wondered that if in her tired state if she turned on the music, or if it was her automatic alarm. Either way she was not very concerned as she continued to wash her hair.

She heard the bathroom door open and now begins to exhibit some anxiety. She attempts to wash the lather out of her face, but it is too late.

Will flung the shower curtain back, which allowed the water to spray outside of the tub; he then stepped in and clutched her by the neck. She could not see him because of the lather in her eyes, and the position she had been facing. She was startled, but not afraid. He continued to enter into the shower, pressing his naked body against hers. Instantly, he rose. She was well aware who invaded her sexual space. She had been at this very place many times before. He turned her around and snatched her body loofah. Roughly, he took the loofah and massaged her delicate skin. It hurt, but she did not want him to stop. She just calmed his roughness by digging into his chest with her nails that surpassed his roughness. He picked her up by her legs and mounted her on the shower wall. He then gave the bird a place to perch. As he penetrated, she gave in and tasted the lather that stung his chest. The shower was quick, but not so quick, that she was left dissatisfied...After the cleansing, the lust continued into the bedroom. He carried her into the bedroom, water still running, only to finish *doing the damn thang,* he had come to do.

There was an uneasy silence about the two of them. An awkward silence, a silence that begged for conversation.

"How is your wife?" She asks with the appearance of superficial guilt

"How can you ask a question like that at a time like this? You really do the craziest shit," he said, projecting his guilt with anger.

"Well, she *is* my sister," she replied.

"Well, why don't you go see her, instead of asking me dumb assed questions?" He stated with just as much emphasis as she had chimed, then he goes to turn off the running water.

"I will in the morning!" she yelled.

After turning off the water, his hunger demands he display an affect much different than the one he showed upon his return.

"Honey, did you bring some food home from the job?"

"Go get it. It's in the car," she responded.

"Why didn't you bring it in?"

"I was too tired."

"Where's Kandesia?" he asked changing the subject.

"She is spending the night at a friend's house."

"Do you think she should be?" he asked concerned.

"Do you think *you should be?*…What am I to say to her Will? Please, you tell me."

She looks at him more intensely than he at her. He surrenders, and just looks away as he asks, "Is she coming to the hospital tomorrow?"

"She said she would, but she didn't make plans with me. I guess she'll get there on her own. Anyway, I plan to get there early so that I can speak with the doctor."

"Well, how early is early?" he asked slyly.

"Are you going to get the food or what?" she responds ignoring his attempt to make plans to satisfy his sex organ just before going to the hospital.

He went into the parking garage and brought in the food. He re-warmed the food and devoured it like a savage. Saving nothing for her. When he returned to the bedroom, he asked, "Were you hungry?"

Knowing him, she knew there was nothing left for her. She asked, "What difference does it make Will? Really."

She wasn't hungry, but wanted him to know ignorant questions were not welcomed.

He turned on the television and listened to the news. "The famous chess grandmaster…more to come at eleven…" the newscaster reported.

Thinking of her sister with tears in her eyes, she began to fall asleep. He turned off the television. Oblivious to her mood and the tears in her eyes, in a cuddling manner spooned her.

Thinking that he is being sensitive to her needs, she turns around to talk.

"Are you crying?" he said in a manner of total surprise.

Realizing that she had been hoodwinked and he being concerned with the true reason behind her tears was wishful thinking, she turned back around, and slid over to her edge of the bed.

He makes a move to penetrate her a second time just before she falls into a good night's sleep. Thinking of her sister, she rejects his advance.

They both roll over and get some rest. In the morning, he slipped out before Kandesia returned home.

At the University medical Center in Las Vegas…

The doctors were overwhelmed with the patient load. At the team meeting, they discussed the alternatives to the managed plan of care. There were significant problems in the units. One challenge that was discussed was that the hospital has not been successful in decreasing the workload without decreasing the census.

UMC is the major trauma center for the city. The emergency vehicles send most of their cases to this hospital. The nurses have been overworked and bitter for an extended period. Not because of the patient load, they are used to a high patient load, but because it continues to get worse. If they handle a load of twenty critical patients with five nurses, then the administrator gives us a desktop computer at the nurses' station for Christmas and says that you can do it with four. Merry Christmas.

This meeting went on for at least two hours. Most of the doctors didn't even care they just wanted to do what they did best, take care of the patients. Let the management handle the census problem. The concerted feeling among attending medical doctors was there wasn't enough staff. The director of medicine and the director of nursing felt the same way. They just couldn't reach the administrator. If they didn't make a miracle happen, then they were in danger of losing their jobs. They were afraid to complain because nurses were being replaced with computers. The loss of their reputation was also at stake. After the meeting, they had lunch that was already prepared and sent up to them by dietary. The dietary section did not prepare the food. They hired catering staff.

"Did you hear what Dr. Williams said to me this week?" Gillianne complains while sitting at the nurses' station. He thinks that I am not culturally sensitive to the patients' needs and says that I need to be educated on holistic medicine. See what happens when a black man gets a position. I almost told him to kiss my black ass!"

"But you like your job," the head nurse said with a smile. The nurses cackle at the front desk.

"How can you like a job that is gonna send you to the mental house?" Gillianne responds.

"You mean we are not there already?" Another nurse chimes in.

"I thought I was yesterday…did you hear Mrs. Sapphire last evening? She is whacked out…saying run, run, Candy, run sweet thing or he's gonna kill you. You are not alone in that train. She then started shrieking OHH MY GOD!!! OH MY GODDDD! We thought she was dying that night, we called the MD and he ordered restraints and a "put er' out" cocktail.

"What's that?"

You know the "2-5-50."

"Ohhh, 2mg ativan, 5 mg haldol, and the 50mg of benadryl."

It was a shot directly to the gluteus. She received two cocktails. If I would have only given her one, it would have just made her notice me, and I'll be damned if I wanted that. She is scary."

Demaci, a single Latino male nurse over-concerned with everyone's appearance especially his, walks in on the tail end of the conversation. Demaci is a little (meaning a lot) on the feminine side. He enters the nurse's station after completing all of the dressings he was asked to do.

"Demaci, did you finish the catherization of the coma patient?" The head nurse asks.

"Of course I finished everything I was told to do, except that. You are running me like an African slave. I think you should know I'm Puerto Rican. Look at me, I'm sweating all over," Demaci returned fanning himself, although he had not a drop of sweat upon him.

"The head nurse responds with an attitude, well I am Puerto black, now straight cath that patient in room 112 before Dr. Herst gets back."

"Puerco Black, ohh I didn't know." Only the Latin nurses seemed to get it, but they didn't let on to the others that he had just called the head nurse a black pig.

"Dr. Herse, Dr. Herse…who in the hell would go to a doctor named Dr. Herse. That's probably why all of his patients are in comas. Why don't they just put a Foley in this guy anyways? He's incontinent," Demaci tirades with his hands moving and his lisp gradually becoming more and more noticeable.

"We need a signed consent form and we don't have one. His family should be coming to speak with the doctor today."

"Thank God, mommi because I am tired of fondling this man," Demaci said. "No you're not," another nurse retorts on time. The station begins to laugh again.

At this time, Dr. Herst walks on the floor. The first thing he asks, "Is the patient in 112 cathed? I want to have him prepped and ready for the procedure at 1300." No one responds to Dr. Herst, not even Demaci. He just bolts out to get the equipment.

In room 112...

In room 112, the doctor consulted with Mr. Sapphire regarding the condition of his wife. The other family members had visited, prayed and left by this time. Although there were five people in the room, it remained cold and lonely. The visitors eventually became comfortable with the somber beeps and blips of the monitor alarms. Abnormal readings accounted for most of the background noise, but to many family members, *my loved one is still alive,* is what was heard. Close by, behind the curtain, was a patient in a coma.

Looking out the window, the black clouds make the middle of the day seem like the evening. The air smells like rain, but the rain has not penetrated these black clouds. The thunder rolls, but the lightning is distant, just like the rainwater.

The beds are clean, but uninviting. Because the mortality rate had been increasing, the community seemed to have lost trust. Even with the lack of confidence, UMC hospital still received the highest volume of patients in their radius.

"Mr. Sapphire, I think it is time to call the family and tell them to get here as soon as they can, her condition is worsening, unless something miraculous happens, she won't survive the night," Dr. David Williams stated monotonically.

Mrs. Sapphire begins to mumble..."You did not stop the beast. The beast is still living. You have got to kill the beast!" Her voice deepens like that of a madman, and she growls, "The existence of the world depends on it." She starts to laugh inappropriately.

"What is she talking about?" Mr. Sapphire inquired.

"I have no idea," Dr. Williams replied. "She has been rambling incoherently since yesterday evening. It's called organic brain syndrome, due to significant trauma to the cerebral region, which is manifested by altered mental status. We have given her oxygen, however it did not improve. This is a serious condition. This is one of the reasons we felt the need to call the family."

Mr. Sapphire called the family...

"Kandesia put your mother on the phone...Janice call the family and tells them to get here at once the doctor says she may not make it through the night."

"Well why didn't he tell us that when we were there?" She screamed. "We would have never gone home. Freakin quack!" Janice cried uncontrollably over the line loud enough for the doctor to overhear.

Dr. Williams pretended that he did not hear her statement as Mr. Sapphire tried to cover the earpiece to prevent any more projected lashings.

"Err, I don't know Janice, but please do that for me. I will call my side of the family," Mr. Sapphire said curtly and hung up before she could have another chance to vent.

When the family finally arrives, Dr. Williams allowed them to come in five at a time. Usually, only two visitors at a time were allowed to visit. Dr. Williams made an exception for this particular circumstance.

The visit consisted of Mr. Sapphire, Mrs. Sapphire's sister Janice, Janice's daughter Kandesia, and Mr. Sapphire's Brother and his brother's wife. Mr. Sapphire welcomes the rest of the family members that just entered the room with a hug and a kiss.

Mrs. Sapphire is staring up at the ceiling with just the whites of her eyes visible. Her torso is arched towards the ceiling also. Her voice changes to a little child now.

"Please don't kill mommy! Daddyyyyyy!" she screams. Then she starts to seize and goes into status epilepticus.

The nurse gave her 10mg of diazepam via IV slow push stat.

"She has to be sedated and restrained. Get the orderlies in here at once and restrain her," Dr. Williams blurted out rhythmically.

In a few moments, she was relaxed; however, her pupils continue to be hidden. She is smiling inappropriately. She begins to speak again. "What brings you here? You want to fuck my husband, *again*? Hahaha. You thought you both could keep a secret.....Well I have a secret that I have been keeping! Dr. Williams was chosen to keep me alive. He is the best in the country...well, I hope that he can prove it. I will die on this bed on the night of the morrow. My death will trigger the release some souls that will curse your children and bring havoc upon this world," and with that breath, she fainted.

"What is going on here...Will, *what* is Vanesia talking about?" Asks his brother Joey, with a distained look on his face.

"She's insane. She has lost her mind. God help her," Mr. Sapphire responds.

"Joey, I think I am ready to go," Sharon says to her husband in disgust, staring at Janice and Will shamefully.

"Sharon, we really should...." Janice is interrupted by Sharon, "Save it Janice, please. How could you...I mean really, how could you.... to your *own sister!*"

Janice's affect exhibited total embarrassment. It was appropriate to the way she had been feeling.

Will exclaimed, "Nothing happened Sharon, now cut it out!"

"Joe, let's go!" Sharon demanded.

"I thought we would all leave together and get something to eat," Joe replied.

"I don't feel hungry...personally I am feeling sick." And with that, Sharon walked out. Joe followed her out.

Demaci was in the room at bed B. While this contentious conversation was played out, no one even noticed him. He noticed them however. Although the procedure normally took ten minutes, he extended the procedure to ascertain that he consumed all that was said. After hearing it all, he finished the procedure and left.

Everyone departed except Kandesia. Kandesia conveniently fell asleep in the chair next to her aunt's bedside. When she awoke, it was about 11:30 pm. Kandesia was nervous...nervous because she didn't know how to tell her aunt something that she had been hiding for about ten weeks. At the age of twenty and in her third year of college, she wanted to tell her aunt everything she had experienced recently. She loved Aunt Vanesia with all of her heart, but she was also embarrassed. She could have easily been embarrassed about what Aunt Vanesia said about mother and uncle, but she wasn't. It was not a question of belief. Although they said that Aunt Vanesia was touched in the mind. Kandesia always suspected that the two of them (her mom and her uncle) were "cheatin' in the next room."

"Aunt Vanesia, I have something to tell you," Kandesia said.

Vanesia opened her eyes and sat up erect. With a voice of a witch, and the tone mutated like she was speaking into a fan in slow motion, she began to moan.

"Mmmmmpphhh...you want to tell me you are with child...a tiny...little.... baby boy." Aunt Janice then started laughing inappropriately. "I have something to tell you, she said in a spooky voice. You have three souls in your womb, not one."

Kandesia *was* pregnant.

How did she know? And how did she know it was a boy? I didn't even know it was a boy. Kandesia thought to herself. She was skeptical about having three children in her belly. After all, the doctor said she was pregnant; not that she was having triplets. He would have told her if this were true. All of a sudden, it stated to rain. Aunt Vanesia threw herself back on the bed and began to cry.

Kandesia was scared. She had never seen her aunt act so strangely.

"Auntie don't cry, please.... I will be ok. I promise, but you are scaring me."

At that moment, her aunt stopped crying, but there was continuous thunder and lightning. Blankets of rain and wind were hitting the window hard enough to break through.

"I will come back tomorrow. I love you auntie," she said with conviction.

"If you leave today, I will not see you again in this life. You will return tomorrow, it will not be to see me." And with that, she fell victim to narcolepsy.

Kandesia, worried about Aunt Vanesia's health, went up to the nurses station and told the nurse what her Auntie had said.

"Please check on her because she doesn't feel as if she is gonna make it."

Demaci had a knack for helping people find piece in mourning. He walked over to Kandesia, held her hand and said to her peacefully, "Your aunt was and still is a very strong woman, but there are times when the body says, I have had enough. Your aunt has significant health problems. I am not sure if the doctor told you, but your aunt is presently a candidate for hospice. He has considered her condition terminal and in the end stages. Now we will do all that we can to make her stay with us as pleasant and comfortable as we can," Demaci says. His tone although the same, expresses more sensitivity as he stated, "Kandesia, she also has a mental disturbance, that is organic...so when she says certain things, you have to understand that she is not herself at times."

Kandesia understood, so she thought, and thanked him for his kind truth. She did not return to the room; instead, she decided to begin the journey in the inclement weather. Knowing she did not have enough money to take a cab, she would have to take public transportation.

Chapter XXVI

That night, Kandesia tried desperately to get home. She wanted tell her boyfriend all that occurred during the conversation with her aunt. He had called her several times, but received the answering machine. It was the rule in the hospital to turn of all cell phones. Kandesia was a law-abiding citizen, especially when it came to her auntie's health. It was about twelve thirty in the morning. The rain came down harder than ever and she was drenched. The umbrella that she brought with her did not last the second weather lashing. On the fourth stair, as she exited the hospital, the umbrella reverses upon itself. She makes a diligent effort to regain her umbrella. The more she tries, the wetter she gets.

Although dressed like a student, her curves told a different story. Her buxom body being enhanced by the raindrop silhouette, she looked more like an entertainer than a postgraduate bound student.

Kandesia finally arrived at the train station. The city was cutting back on booth attendants, but they considered the cameras an inexpensive replacement. She went to the machine, shuffled through her purse and purchased a metrocard. She went through the turnstile to the platform and waited for the train to arrive. When the train entered the station, she got on the train. Concerned with her pre-occupation of her boyfriend hearing the news, she failed to check the car for safety. It was not empty. This car hosted a group of thugs. They had already robbed others and scared a few out of the car.

As she sits down, she heard the clamor of delinquent youth. She noticed the group of guys. They were getting high at the other end of the car. Regaining her wit about her, she gets a book out of her purse and pretends to be reading it. She can tell that the gang has spotted her, but she didn't want to be conspicuous. She gets up and begins to walk to another car. The undesirables follow her. She tries to get through the car door but it is locked. As she turns around to find a seat closer to the door, a young punk blocks her path. She was face to face with him as he attempts to force her into conversation...

"Hey mami, what's good?" One of the guys said to her while he combed his half corn roll half-afro hairdo, split straight down the middle. Kandesia does not respond.

"Ohhh, you can't speak? You too good to holla at the kid?" She continued to ignore him, as she moved around the pick, and took a seat. She then pretended to read her book. He grabbed the book and threw it to the back of the car.

She shrieks at the top of her lungs, "What in the hell..." but before she could finish her statement she is grabbed around her neck by another gang member.

"Shut your mouth freak!" he said ruthlessly. Then they began checking her pockets. They groped her as they checked for money. What began from a simple robbery escalated to a violation worthy of a life sentence.

"Please you guys, it is not worth it, just take my money...PLEASE JUST TAKE MY MONEY. JUST TAKE THE MONEY...I AM PREGNANT!" She emptied out the contents of her purse to them. They were not interested in the lack of money she had in her purse. They tore her wet clothes off her upper body.

"Damned, you look good for a pregnant chick," one thug said. The fact that she was pregnant seemed to turn them on.

At this point, she was delirious. She knew that any attempt to escape was futile. No one with chivalry heard her cries, the few cowards that did hear her cry, pretended that they didn't. One man in particular got on the train, saw the incident in progress, then stepped off the train, hoping that no one noticed him. Instead of calling the authorities, he just got on the next train and thanked God that he wasn't the victim.

Two to three minutes seemed like an hour. She is raped and sodomized by two of the gang members. After they had their way with her, they beat her senseless. She could no longer stand up. The train arrived at the next station. They threw her on the platform and left her for dead. It was not apparent to her that she had been stabbed when she tried to resist the violation. Half naked, she crawled, bleeding internally from the abdomen, until she went unconscious. She was found sometime in the early morning and rushed to the hospital, the same hospital where her aunt was admitted.

When Kandesia finally arrived, the reporters were there. They were not there for her, but because of her auntie. They were getting the stories of her premonitions. They were talking about the affair her mother had with her uncle; although Kandesia was unconscious, she heard everything that they said, when she knew that her personal business was going to be public, she lost the will to live. She thought about what her aunt had said to her before she left. *"If you leave today, I will not see you again in this life. You will return tomorrow, it will not be to see me."* She knew now what her aunt had meant; only she realized it too late.

She felt death overcome her. She had all of these preconceived notions of what death was, and she was wrong. It was not painful. Living was, but death was not. It felt strange. Not because it was an eerie feeling, but because it was nothing she had expected. It was peaceful. Although it was serene and she welcomed it, she wished that she could speak with her auntie one last time. She died displaying a horrific facial expression while being transported on the stretcher. Her face was congruent with the beating and the pain of life, but not with the transition and the tone of death. They took her directly into the surgical room. Dr. Williams's best team worked on her, but no one could save her...not even Dr. Williams.

Once Demaci told his story to the press, the media camped out at the hospital. The press began to interview Vanesia Sapphire. At times, she was coherent, at other times she was not. But at all times the prophecy was given.

"Mrs. Sapphire is it true that you can see things?" One reporter inquired.

"It is true," she growls and laughs inappropriately.

"Well, I must say that some of the people don't believe in your fortune telling," he responded.

Just then, Demaci comes in to complete the passive range of motion and turn his coma patient. He sees the reporter and tells him that he must leave. Mrs. Sapphire stops the reporter and speaks...

"Wait! He must not leave and neither you until you know. Mr. Demaci, do you realllly know your patient?"

"Not reallly, really like all his personal information," he responded just as she had spoken to him.

At that moment, she received a vision. The sky turned colors and the rain began to fall. She went into a trance. At once, everyone backed away from her. The reporter cues his camcorder. "Did you know that he is a grandmaster chess player?" She revealed with her sclera in full view.

And again, Demaci responds in the negative.

As she was speaking, the reporter was jotting all of it down verbatim.

"Well, soon that man will be the recipient of a miracle. He will escape from the dungeon, the dungeon that has held his soul hostage for the years that past. He will soon be alert; however, he will never be the same man that he was before.

He will be institutionalized in a psychiatric hospital, and he will be stung by a bee, a great bee, the Queen of all Bees." The volume of her voice climaxes as she completed her sentence. She falls into an irreversible seizure and dies.

The board screams in unison with Tye in the hospital bed, "NOOOOOO!"

This story was in the papers for a long time. Mr. Sapphire could not live a peaceful life; the reporters would be at the estate everyday, asking him uncomfortable questions. He had to relocate. Everywhere Mr. Sapphire went the reporters followed. He went to the courts to change his name. He obtained a marriage license and married Janice. They changed their names…. To the Barnsworth's.

Seven is a righteous number. Four plus three equals seven. If you haven't guessed…three is the number that must return the demons to Hell.

Chapter XXVII

Mr. James lets out this sick laugh, and speaks out in a voice very different than his own. I have enjoyed your stories…I really have, but it is time for me to do a little sharing with you. Boy, do you know who I am?

"I do. You are the demon named Demitri that is possessing Mr. James," stated Roman in a calm and balanced voice.

"And you still entertain me!?" Demitri responds angrily as if he were insulted.

"I do. You are the last demon to return to hell," responds Roman, but this time his voice is quivers a bit.

"Boy you don't know me, *but you're about to get to know me!*" Demitri growls like a wild animal. The bar began to quake, and his wife slipped out to the back room and locked the door between her and them, providing a false sense of safety.

"Demitri, I…I…I am just a young boy cursed by his dreams. Please don't take your anger out on me. I just dream…I have no control over what has already been determined in the scrolls of life," Roman stuttered in acceleration. It is evident that he is terrified as he got himself up and eased towards the door, refusing to turn his back on Demitri…

"Enough about the ssscrolls of me, what about scrollsss of you?" Demitri hissed, as he followed Roman.

"I have not read the scrolls, but my dreams show me protected."

"You place too much faith in your dreams boy," he hissed as his tongue changes to the forked tongue of a serpent. Demitri used his mind to close all of the doors that were once open.

Just at that moment, out of the blue, Roman gets some help from Sirius, his Angel of protection as he encounters the beast.

And you take them too lightly demon! Sirius retorts as he flung the door open allowing Roman to get a head start, making a hasty exit.

"I know you," hissed the demon. "You have walked this earth before…you are Sirius, The Angel of Restitution."

And I know you. You are a baron of hell. They call you Demitri, Sirius responded.

"So you must also know that you alone are no match for me," Demitri added.

I am not here to aggress. I am here to protect. I have done my job. There will be others like me to hunt you down and restore your soul to hell. Just as Sirius appeared, he also left.

Demitri took Mr. James's worn body and ran out the door, attempting to take flight just as Roman had, looking for any glimpse of the child. Roman was breaking track records. There would be no catching him utilizing Mr. James's legs. The beast then left the body of Mr. James, and literally took flight searching for Roman. He wanted to hear the rest of the dream. He needed to know how he could combat the prophecy. Roman had taken a short cut, entering the subway. He took the exit that lead him to the other side of Queens Blvd, also known as *the Boulevard of Death*. He continued at that pace. A pace that could only be attained fueled by adrenalin, until he reached his building. Demitri was close behind as he soared through the air.

As Roman entered the building, Demitri was already in the staircase. Roman, not waiting for the elevator, ran up the steps. He tried to reach the ninth floor before he could be detected. He did not make it.

"Boy you must know I need the end of the prophecy! And I will not leave without getting the answer. Do not make this difficult. I may not have the power to take life…but I do have the power to make it so unbearable that you will take your own!" And with that, the beast had placed these pruritic warts all over Roman's body. They were hideous. Roman attempted to ease the sensation by scratching himself all over his body.

"What are you doing to me? I have nothing to do with this! I just have the dreams, OK? Why must you torture me? I am just a messenger. These dreams are a curse to me," Roman says.

Demitri begins to lose patience with his chatter. He starts to ignite the warts so that they burn the insides of Roman.

"Helllp! Help me! Ahhhhh!" He screams in horror. No one hears his cry.

Just as he is screaming, a few of his female schoolmates enter the staircase with their ipods blasting the eardrums. La Shawn, a particular female to whom he is attracted, and her girlfriend, Brittany notices Roman. She observes what she interprets to be Roman talking to himself and looks at him very strangely...She then walks backwards up the stairs, hoping not to be noticed, and Brittany follows. They sit at the elevator for a moment and Brittany taps LaShawn, to get her attention. LaShawn removes her earpiece.

"Damn La Shawn, your boyfriend is a cornball, and needs to do something about that bumpy face!" Brittany yells to her as she removes her earpiece.

"Roman's not my boyfriend!" La Shawn responds in an angry, embarrassed tone.

LaShawn presses the down button third time, trying to place a rush on the slow elevators.

Roman, defeated and mortified, gives up.

"Okay, Okay, I will tell you," Roman says painfully. He knelt in exhaustion and told the ending of his dream.

"I dreamt that three were returned to hell. That was the prophecy. The only way you can change the prophecy is to locate four demons that have escaped the depths of hell. Subvidious, Anglore, Tempest, and Curmis. If you can get them to form an alliance with you, you will be able to go to war with Sirius! This is the only way you shall be able to combat the Angel of Restitution. He has been summoned to return you to hell!"

"Why do I need these demons to combat Sirius? He is no match for me!" Demitri says in an attempt to sharpen the blades of his courage.

"Sirius is more powerful than you may have imagined. He is not to be underestimated. If you do not have the alliance of all four of these demons, you are sure to return to hell. Now please release me from this burning skin disease." With a wave of his hand, Demitri released him from the affliction.

Roman runs up the stairs to the ninth floor through the hallway, where strangely all of the lights are working. He bangs on the door until his brother opens it. He rushes past his family at the dining room table, and goes directly to the bedroom. He completes his ritual, grabs his pills, swallows a few down whole and prays. He jumps in the bed without eating dinner and goes fast to sleep.

Since this had happened many times before, they do not disturb him. They attribute his behavior to his psych issues. As they chalked his behavior up to just another episode, his family returns to their dinner without an investigation.

"Mom was he adopted?" Asks Shawn as he reaches for the broccoli.

"Shut up," retorts the father.

Roman's family continued to eat and talk about what happened throughout the day.

Demitri returned to his lair. He went through his personal books of the secret arts of the crafts, and summoned the demons one by one in a séance. The chants began and the first demon that appeared was Curmis, then appeared Anglore…after a while appeared Subvidious. Demitri received three of the four demons. Tempest was as strong as she was wise, and would not appear. Demitri explained the prophecy to the other demons and requested their help to retrieve her. Demitri further explained that if they will not join him in the defense, they would surely be hunted down one by one and returned to hell. After speaking with Demitri, they were sure of what they needed to do. They needed to find Tempest.

Since the other three demons knew where Tempest was dwelling they set out to capture her.

It did not take long to find her…she had possessed a woman in a hospital telling of various prophecies that were to come to pass. Tempest was grabbed out of the woman by the demons. They had been trying to exorcise Tempest from this woman for hours. But Tempest was powerful. It took the strength of all four of them to exorcise the demon out of the lady, but after they did, the lady had a seizure and died. Tempest's spirit had been keeping the woman alive. Now that Tempest had left the body, Vanesia could not withstand death's calling.

"You fools! What are you doing?" Tempest said in a rage.

"You must hear the prophecy," Demitri said.

"I know of Subvidious, I know Anglore, I even know Curmis…But who are you, and why have you summoned our demise?"

"I am Demitri. And what demise do you envision?" he said.

"I do not see all, but I do see enough to say that you fools should have let me be," Tempest stated as she cracked her whip. Curmis and Anglore subdue Tempest. Although you could not see the force, she was imprisoned by it, and caused to listen.

"I do not wish to fight…I wish to save us from our fate," Demitri explained.

"Save yourselves!" she bellowed.

"Silence her," Demitri said. Her mouth was removed, and she was left with no orifice to speak. While she looked on in a bewildered state, he then made Tempest listen to the prophecy from the beginning.

Chapter XXVIII

As Roman slept, his nightmare became worse. Uncontrollably he shook, but he could not awaken. Sweating profusely, he embraces the dream. Over and over in his nightmare, he witnesses Sirius getting worked over by the very spirits that he first dreamt. Sirius was making a valiant attempt to ward off the demons, but in this dream, Sirius was on the losing end of this battle. Sirius took his blade, and swung it like the hammer of Thor. Just before he caught the beast with the blade, no one know exactly what happened, but Roman was placed in the position to receive the blow, and the demon was no where to be found. The blow sliced Roman's neck in half. Roman looked at Sirius in shock and fell to his knees. He held in a grip…a grip that could best be described as the universal choking sign, what was left of his neck. His head rolled onto the floor. His eyes and mouth continued to be wide open as the head traveled to the feet of Sirius.

Roman sat up in his bed, clutching his neck and trying desperately to awaken, but the hag would not release him to the conscious state. Roman futilely trying to regain consciousness fell back onto the pillow in exasperation. Once again, Sirius appeared in his dreams. This time he bought a message. "You have done well my young one. You have done well." As roman continued to dream, the shaking subsides.

Sirius uses his celestial abilities to search for the clan. As he searched the universe with his mind, he found the clan, and their lair. Sirius entered into the lair and found the demons plotting.

None of the demons notice his presence at first. They continue plotting until Tempest began to sense something. As her meta-olfactory curiosity increased, her nostrils flared. She begins to pick up a foreign scent. Still no one pays attention to her inquiry. As she begs with her eyes to be released from the spell, the intruder finds his way into the lair. Suddenly Curmis picks up on her plea and allows his hold on her bondage and her mouth to be released. Effortlessly, she suspends what is left of the warlock craft they had impressed upon her.

"You fools do not know what you have done! There is something in here!" Tempest whispers as loud as she could manage.

Whatever was in there obviously was not more important than the conversation they were having. While they continue to talk, she leaves the conversation. Edging easily around the lair as a hunting dog scenting out a quail. Finally the others pick up on her intuition, but only she and she alone, knew that there was an intruder in their midst. Although she could not place the menace, it did not sit right with her. Tempest continued to follow her sixth sense. She crept right up to Sirius as he could not be detected by sight, and instantly she jumps back…far to the other side of the lair, and plants herself onto the wall near the stained glass window. She reveals her whip and snaps it to display her defense.

"Sirius your fool. You come here alone?" Demitri growls. All the demons are able to see Sirius now that they are aware he is in cloak. He attacks Sirius with a force that came from his hand. Sirius takes the sword out of his chamber spins around, kneels down in a warrior's stance, and blocks the force with his sword aligned with his back, his back facing Demitri, and his front facing Tempest.

Tempest jumps into the fight by lassoing him in with her whip as she wrapped it around his neck. Tempest had a very strong evil force. She was as strong as Demitri, but much more evil. As she controls him by the neck with her whip, Sirius, Anglore, and Subvidious try to unman his weapon. They are unsuccessful. Before they can cause any pain the doors and windows fly open, and at each opening, there is a light. Instantly the demons hold on Sirius is released and they are all suspended against the wall.

"What is this? The prophecy said that you could not combat us all!" Demitri cries.

"You did not hear the entire prophecy. The end of the prophecy states that four were released, Subvidious, Anglore, Curmis and Tempest. It then states it would take three to return them. You, Roman, and myself. I thank you for your assistance in bringing them to hell."

Tempest is wily at this point. The same bewildered look overcame her.

"You will rue this day Demitri. You will rue this day, I swear it!" Tempest says with a snarl as she spat a lungy next to his feet. She then recites a demonic curse in an ancient language, unrecognizable to the modern English ear. The other demons spew the same nasty curses in unison…in Demitri's direction. The chant became louder and not only is Demitri ashamed of his ignorant behavior, but he is also terrified for what punishment his ignorant behavior may have consequenced.

"What about me?" Demitri asks.

"You will return also," Sirius responds.

"You can't be serious. You alone are no match for me," Demitri laughs nervously.

"Ohh. I will prove to you just how Sirius I am," Sirius replies confidently.

"It would be difficult for me to bring you to hell alone, as my strength to do so is questionable, but since you helped me take Subvidious, Anglore, Curmis, and Tempest to hell. And their sentence is final. I am certain that they won't have a problem taking you with them."

Tempest wraps her whip around Demitri's neck and pulls him to close to her. She licks his neck; it burns like hellfire, just to give him a foretaste of the agony he is about to endure. Anglore and Curmis grab each extremity of Demitri's lanky body, as Subvidious envelops the entire team like a ball and entraps Demitri so he could not escape.

"NOOOOOOOO!" Demitri cries aloud, as he is thrusted into hell, not passing go and not collecting two hundred dollars.

Epilogue

Ms. Adaire's hand written letter read:

Dear Mr. and Mrs. Phoenix,

I hope that this letter finds you in the best of health and prosperity. I have written a letter to all of my chess team parents. Please take the time to read the entire letter as it took a lot for me to write it. There are two reasons I have taken the time to write you. The first has to do with the following request. I am asking all of the parents to give me fifty dollars to purchase jackets that have the school logo and the chess team embroidered on the jacket pocket. I know this is costly, but it would be worth it. I do not expect them to be grand masters or even win every game, but I do expect them to learn something...learn something about life strategies, pride in themselves and the love of friendship. I am proud of our chess team and want them to look professional. If you cannot afford the full price, give what you can and I will see to it that they are wearing a personalized jacket during the competition.

The second reason is a bit harder for me to write. It involves a condition that I have recently accepted and am comfortable enough to share with you. I hope that my words are not taken in any way but the way that they were intended. Roman, is a blessed child. He is clearly different from others. I know, because I take time to appreciate my students. I can't even say why, but I can relate to him. He really cares about people. Roman came to me in the beginning of the semester and said he dreamt about me. He seemed to be worried. Something told me not to handle this in the normal fashion. I felt a little awkward. Not knowing what he was going to say, I asked him what he dreamt. He told me he dreamt that I was happy. Subsequently, he asked me if I was happy. I was honest with him and I told him no. Roman smiled. He seemed relieved that I was not happy. He then told me that in his dream, I was happy, but dying. At the end of his dream, I was in a casket. I was dressed in a black suit that had *Coach-The Strategists* on the jacket pocket. At the time neither one of us knew what that meant. He may have forgotten, but I did not. His prophecy was coming to pass. His only concern was that if I was happy then I was ready to die. Well, I was not happy then, because my results came back from the doctor that day. The tests confirmed that I had cancer. Somehow, Roman knew this even before I did. Thirty-eight years old and I was told that I am dying of breast cancer. It has since then spread to my lungs. So of course, I was not happy.

Being an educator, you learn that knowledge is not only found in a school-book. Just as I was teaching, I was being taught…taught about life, love, and true happiness. I never knew that coaching a chess team would be so much fun, and bring so satisfaction to my life. God places people in your life for a reason. I needed you and my students, especially the chess team. I needed you to make me smile, to make me laugh, I know now that laughter is the best medicine. I needed you to feel appreciated. Thank you. God has allowed me to see the brilliance of life. Some people go their entire lives without seeing the beauty. He has allowed me to see it everyday. For that, I am blessed. I can truly say that I am happy now. I know that I do not have long to live. I would like to live long enough to see our children graduate. Although I wish I had more time, I am ready for what is next. If you live long enough, you realize that all good things you know never last.

Most importantly, I do not want the children to know about my condition. Second matter of importance is that I want the children to be surprised when they come to the tournament. So please do not tell them about the jackets.

PS—Tangie, I never thought that I would say this, but I do have favorite students…they are my chess team.

The strategists took home the first place district trophy, and took second in the state. Ms. Adaire was able to see the results of the seeds she sowed. In the final semester, just before graduation, the battle with cancer ended. Ms. Adaire had passed with flying colors. She had graduated this place with a smile on her face.

Her funeral had been on a Saturday afternoon.

The day of graduation came shortly after. Without Ms. Adaire, the auditorium did not look regal as it once had. And with family and friends along the aisles, in folding chairs, even standing along the walls, the auditorium appeared smaller. The turnout was still incredible. The faculty did a spectacular job orchestrating the graduation. There was a roar of conversation. Families tried to find their young graduates, who were seated in the front by classroom, and in alphabetical order. The only difference in seating arrangements had to do with Ms. Adaire's chess team. We all sat together. We were present and looking appropriate, as Ms. Adaire would have liked.

The principal had risen to say a few words in honor of the graduating class. He also said a few words on behalf of Ms. Adaire. We had a moment of silence in her honor. Also, in honor of Ms. Adaire, the chess team graduated in their uniforms.

After the graduation, the graduating class and their families assembled in the gymnasium. The Parent Teacher Association set up a lovely reception area in the gymnasium. Although the gym was normally the same size as the auditorium, it was expandable. A removable divider had been placed in the center of the gym. Once opened, it made the gym twice its original size.

As the graduates trickled into the auditorium with their families, pictures of Ms. Adaire with her students were being displayed onto the far wall of the gymnasium. After the slide show of Ms. Adaire and her students, I noticed some of our chess team pictures being displayed. A final picture of Ms Adaire was projected on the wall. Although it was in spirit, she *was* able to see us graduate. Her presence was felt throughout the auditorium.

Venus de Milo was playing, one of Ms. Adaire's favorite songs. It was appropriate, because her beauty, like *The Venus de Milo*, had touched many hearts.

About the Author

Greetings to all. I was born in Queens, New York City. I reside in Brooklyn, and work in a hospital in the same community.

I also wrote a book entitled, *Minutes in Morality,* using my professional name, Charles Anthony Ancrum. This book explained stress management techniques and my personal views on how to *get back to the basics.*

I have a long list of things I enjoy, but I will keep this one short. The taste of a fine cognac, a heavenly woman, a good game of chess, and traveling.

Writing is a part of me. I am very affectionate to a fountain pen and quality paper. There is a release that comes from writing. It doesn't matter where I am, I can find inspiration. The reason is because inspiration originates from the inside, not the outside. I resist the urge to slide the jotter from the inside pocket of my suit jacket and record the twist on how I view everyday life. There is just something about looking at someone, smiling, and then writing something down that introduces the hidden paranoia of New Yorkers. Go figure.

Feel Me

Feel me...

Touch me. Not with your hands, but with your heart

The way a hummingbird touches a flower

Kiss Me. Not with your lips, but with your goodness

As a snowflake kisses the tongue of a child

Make me laugh. Not with a joke, but with a tickle

Like the craft of virtuous hands to a belly

Miss me, not with your eyes, but with your soul

The way that I miss you

When we are no longer connected

Feel me?

Again, last but never least, I would like to thank my loyal readers, without you I am just a lonely artist.
I adore you all, God Bless and Take Care.

978-0-595-38579-9
0-595-38579-6

CPSIA information can be obtained at www.ICGtesting.com
Printed in the USA
BVOW021909131111

275915BV00001B/3/A